THE INHERITANCE

To Brian:
Thank you for being a fan.

Sheila Clover

THE INHERITANCE

SHEILA CLOSS

Copyright © 2014 by Sheila Closs.

Library of Congress Control Number: 2014907856
ISBN: Hardcover 978-1-4990-1237-8
Softcover 978-1-4990-1235-4
eBook 978-1-4990-1238-5

All rights reserved. No part of this book may be reproduced or transmitted in any form or by any means, electronic or mechanical, including photocopying, recording, or by any information storage and retrieval system, without permission in writing from the copyright owner.

This is a work of fiction. Names, characters, places and incidents either are the product of the author's imagination or are used fictitiously, and any resemblance to any actual persons, living or dead, events, or locales is entirely coincidental.

Any people depicted in stock imagery provided by Thinkstock are models, and such images are being used for illustrative purposes only.
Certain stock imagery © Thinkstock.

This book was printed in the United States of America.

Rev. date: 04/26/2014

To order additional copies of this book, contact:
Xlibris LLC
1-888-795-4274
www.Xlibris.com
Orders@Xlibris.com
622625

DEDICATION

I would like to dedicate this book to my mother, Helen Miller. She has been an inspiration to me all throughout my life and especially in the trying times. She stands tall and strong to this very day.

CHAPTER ONE

The summer sun was hidden behind a few dark clouds as Dorothy drove past the town limits into Redwood. It was a small city with a population of well over 60,000. That included the cats, dogs, and numerous other small rodents kept as pets. The soft cool breeze seemed to push her along as Dorothy maneuvered her bike past numerous small stores and retail spaces with large glass windows in quaint wooden false front building. She smiled as she remembered the layout of the main street of town. It started at the top of a gradual slope down seven blocks, with hotels, coffee shops, and several small bars spaced along the "main street". The intersections of Main Street were all controlled by four way stop signs back when Dorothy lived here, with more retail shops on the side streets. The top of Main Street held the most breath-taking view of the mountains and forests in between as one looked off to the west.

To go "down" Main Street, one went south and after reaching the bottom, the street curved to the east out to a service road where the first of two street lights had been installed on the intersection crossing the highway that skimmed past Redwood. The other street light was at the intersection of the highway that led to a street going past the high school, some churches, and led one right back to the top of Main Street. This was called "doing the loop". It was a Friday night tradition with teens that had cars to show off with to their friends. Dorothy shook her head and continued to go North up the main street. Memories such as this didn't serve a purpose to Dorothy other than to distract her attention.

Riding a motorbike required more attention than driving a car in Dorothy's experience. Not only did she have to watch for the usual hazards such as pedestrians and small animals, she had to watch for other drivers who seemed to be blind when it came to motorbikes; especially in a small place such as Redwood.

Still, the scene at the top of Main Street made her draw a sharp breath. On a clear day one could see a mountain framed on both sides with smaller mountains, evergreens, blue sky, and soft white clouds. It only took a quick glance for Dorothy to realize how much she wanted to see Redwood again. Turning away from the scene she continued around out to the second half of the loop.

On the one side of the highway was a service road that had service stations in every block. That was one of the perks of a city whose main industries that supported the economy were oil and gas, logging, and farming. Tourist attractions such as a large lake not three miles from the city didn't seem to matter in the winter when the snowdrifts were up to shoulder level and the cold went bone deep.

Dorothy pulled in to the Red Robin gas bar and got off her bike. It was a beautiful Venture with saddle bags, full wind screen, and a radio she was able to hear when she travelled the highway. She kicked the stand and pulled off her full face helmet then shook out her long wavy auburn colored hair. Placing the helmet on the seat she began to pump the gas. A low wheeling older convertible in a canary yellow color pulled up on the other side of the pump. Two little boys immediately began jumping up and down excitedly as they pointed to Dorothy's five foot petite black leather clad body and shouted while they pointed.

"Look Daddy, look! It's a biker. And it's a girl!" They fell back onto the crowded backseat giggling at what they were seeing, as Daddy climbed out of the driver's side and came around to pump his own gas. Dorothy smiled at the two boys before she glanced at the man at the pump beside her. He was a tall man who used to have a heavily muscled athlete's body that was slowly turning to softness and sloppiness. His blond hair was slowly receding but he still wore it in a full mullet style that no longer complimented his heavier features. His eyes were blue and his once good looks were all screwed into a "what I wouldn't do with that" leer Dorothy was all too familiar with. His wife was glancing back over her shoulder and noticed the man's look but turned instead to quiet the two small boys in the back seat.

"*What a winner!*" Dorothy thought to herself. "*Two kids, a wife in the front seat, and he still tries to put the moves on me.*" Dorothy finished with the gas and closed her tank. Stopping at the small trailer hitch she was pulling behind her bike she checked the fittings to make sure it was secure and crossed behind the car to avoid the Romeo and went in to pay her bill.

Behind the counter stood a teenager of average height and familiar features. Dorothy began to grin as she approached the till.

"Hello Billy. How's your Mom and Dad?" Her well modulated tone seemed to stun the young teen into action.

"Aunt Dorothy! You made it! We didn't think you would be bringing your bike though!" Billy came from behind the counter and gave Dorothy a quick hug and then raced out to see the bike sitting on the far side of the pump.

"Wow!" Billy stopped at the rear tire of the bike and ran his hand along the fender and bag. "You did paint it a fire engine red. Dad said you did. Wait until Tiffany sees this!" Tiffany was Billy's girlfriend throughout high school.

In Billy's excitement he forgot all about his other customer who didn't seem pleased with the inattention. His scowl at being ignored made Dorothy shake her head and go back outside.

"Bill. Hey Bill!" The man had to call twice to get his attention.

"Don't I even get a hello now?" The whine in his voice registered his displeasure with Billy.

"Oh hi Mr. Belknap. How are you? You too, Mrs. Belknap." Billy nodded to the lady in the car and received a small smile from Mrs. Belknap for his courtesy. He turned his attention back to the bike and stared in awe. Picking up the helmet he turned to Dorothy with a hopeful smile upon his face. Dorothy laughed.

"Billy, you will never change. I can still read your mind. You'd better come and take my money and settle up with this gentleman before you go playing with my bike." Dorothy turned to go back inside then stopped. Knowing human instinct, she motioned to the helmet. "And bring the helmet in with you, okay?" Dorothy smiled to herself as she sensed the eyes boring into the back of her head from Belknap's direction. Billy was two steps behind Dorothy with the helmet. He placed it reverently on the counter as he rang in Dorothy's gas purchase.

"Dad and mom are already out at the Manor getting ready for everyone's arrival." Billy's brown eyes sparkled with energy as he placed the cash in the drawer and looked up when Belknap walked into the store. Dorothy remained with her back to him as she placed the change into her front pocket. Dorothy sensed Belknap's presence behind her as he placed himself as close to her back as he could without touching her. A bully's trick Dorothy thought to herself. Michael's eyes narrowed and he tensed as if ready to leap over the counter.

Dorothy winked at Billy as she placed the change into her front pocket. She stepped back onto the big toe of Mr. Belknap's right foot with the heel of her boot, grinding her heel in as much as possible. Billy's eyes went wide with concern as Mr. Belknap howled and reached for his leather clad right foot and began to hop around making the worst noise Dorothy ever heard a grown man make.

Belknap stopped hopping and howling and put his foot down gingerly to test his weight on it. Looking up at Dorothy his face began to get red and a sheen of sweat immediately appeared on his florid face.

"I'm sorry. I didn't know you were standing so close." Dorothy said in her most innocent voice while trying not to choke on the laughter bubbling up from inside. "Here. Let me see. Is it hurt badly?" She started to reach forward and down when he jerked back and hopped to go around her to the cash counter.

"Just leave it alone you dumb b—h! Why don't you watch where you're going?" The anger and resentment in his voice began to alarm Billy who involuntarily took a step backwards. Dorothy remained in place.

"Here!" Belknap threw the twenty dollar bill at Billy then turned to leave. "Your father ought to be a little more careful about who he lets into his gas station." He almost bellowed as he began to hop to the door.

"He most certainly should, Billy." Dorothy echoed in a tone of voice that should have been a warning to the man but one he didn't heed. "Some people just don't have any manners."

Belknap turned back around and started to advance towards Dorothy with his fists clenched. Dorothy tensed and readied her stance while her eyes narrowed to mere slits. Her nostrils flared and her body looked deceptively neutral. "*Just raise that fist, man, come on!*" Dorothy thought to herself.

"What did you say little girl?" The bellow came from the bully's mouth as the red flush crept up to the top of his head. Even his hair seemed to stand on end.

At that exact moment a door behind the counter opened and a huge man walked through as if he owned the place and he took in the scene at a glance. He smiled at Dorothy as he came around the end of the counter and enveloped her in a huge bear hug. Belknap's advance had been halted at the appearance of the second man and he now stood rooted to the spot in surprise.

"Dorothy! You're early you little bird you. You weren't supposed to be here until tomorrow!" The man's voice was deep and commanding as Dorothy all but disappeared in his embrace.

"I know, Matt, but I wanted to see the place and go around the loop for old time's sake." Dorothy acknowledged the big man's greeting. "By the way, when did you get the street lights?" She laughed while being held at arm's length.

"Couple years after you left." Matt stepped back to survey Dorothy's leather clad body as a brother would his long lost sister. "Riding the bike, then?" Dorothy nodded.

"I was able to meet some of the locals." Dorothy indicated the now silent and dumb founded Belknap. Billy quietly returned to the till and placed Belknap's money in the tray with a tiny smirk.

"Belknap! How are you today?" Matt's huge frame moved with surprising speed as he placed his arm around the man's should and urged him back towards the counter and Dorothy despite his reluctance. Not waiting for a reply, Matt introduced the two of them.

"Darien Belknap, I would like you to meet my older sister Dorothy Adams. Dorothy, this is Darien Belknap." Matt stood back with a grin on his face.

"We met already." Belknap said after he cleared his throat. "She stepped on my toe on purpose!" He indicated his toe and his actions had the attitude of a hurt little boy showing his boo boo to a parent. Dorothy shook her head once more and began to laugh.

"Sorry, but you were standing fairly close." Dorothy chuckled.

"Yeah, too close!" Billy sided with Dorothy.

"Billy, don't you have some oil to change or windows to wash?" Matt indicated the parking lot with a sweeping gesture of his hand.

"Right! I'm on it Dad!" Billy, Matt's adopted son disappeared out the front door.

"You're his sister?" Darien Belknap struggled to find some kind of indication in the delicate features of Dorothy's face and the bear like face of the man who still stood with his arm draped around his shoulders with a vice like grip.

"Two years older." Dorothy affirmed with a nod of her head.

"She acts more like thirty years older." Matt smiled. "Come over and shake his hand hello." Matt instructed Dorothy. With a withering glance Matt's way, Dorothy took a step forward and extended her hand towards the man who looked like a dwarf compared to Matt's six and a half foot frame. A formidable man when angered or charged with energy for the task at hand, he seemed more like a teddy bear when his wife or his sister were around. In fact, his wife was the only one who could call him a teddy bear to his face but never in public. A horn sounded from outside and Belknap jumped as if jolted out of a trance. Quickly he limply shook Dorothy's hand and scooted out the door.

"Gotta go." Were his only words as he scrambled into his car and drove away in a cloud of dust.

"Dorothy, you should move your bike or bring it in to the bay here and let me tinker with it for a while." Matt urged her to the door as well.

"How about if I just leave the trailer here. Then I will go over to the Inn Hotel for the night. Dorothy placed the helmet on her head and buckled the chin strap.

"I see you can still push some men's buttons like you did before." Matt's laughter spilled out into his eyes. Reading a little bit of reproach in them as well, Dorothy smiled right back at him.

"At least I am in the right this time." Dorothy said as she went out the door into the bright sunlight. The smell of gas, oil, and dust hung in the air as she climbed back onto her bike. It brought back a memory from Dorothy's past. A memory she didn't really want to have anymore. Starting the bike she glanced back to the door of the gas bar. Billy was smiling and waving as he stood beside his dad. "*God how those kids have gotten bigger.*" With a wave and a shoulder check, Dorothy eased back into traffic on the loop. One block past the light, Dorothy pulled into the service road that gave access to the hotel she had booked a room in and found she was glad she had left her trailer at the compound behind the service station. It had been a long dusty ride and Dorothy was looking forward to a nice soft bed to sleep in, a hot tub, and a cold beer. Removing her helmet once more, Dorothy checked the spot where she parked and made sure the bike was secure and out of the way. Pulling a small overnight duffle bag out of a saddle bag of the bike, she pulled a small laptop case out of the other and made her way up the large stone steps and into the lobby of the Inn Hotel. It was the biggest and best in Redwood. Smiling to herself, Dorothy walked up to the front desk. The smiling clerk had just hung up the phone and put a genuine smile on her face as she swept her twenty something blonde hairs out of her eyes.

"Hello, my name is Tiffany."

"*Of course!*" thought Dorothy.

"How may I help you?" Dorothy smiled back at her youthful exuberance. Tiffany looked to be the same age as Billy. Her green uniform vest over a cream blouse with an a-frame skirt made her look modern but stunning as she stood waiting politely for Dorothy to answer.

"I have a reservation for Dorothy Adams." She placed her case and duffle bag at her feet in preparation to sign the guest register. The girl's expression registered instantly to one of complete surprise.

"Is there something wrong?" Dorothy asked Tiffany when she noticed the perfect O made by the girl's lips.

"Uh, no ma'am." The girl hesitated before reaching for the register cards on the counter in front of her. Looking up she gave Dorothy a grin that went from ear to ear. Each pearly white standing out in the slightly tanned face. "It's just that, Billy told me all about you and your adventures and I imagined you to be at least six feet tall like his dad." A touch of excitement came through in her voice. Dorothy started to laugh and shook her head. She should have known.

"Billy never told me you worked here and I just saw him at the station." Dorothy held out her hand. The young girl's surprise lighted her eyes and was quickly replaced with laughter. "Hello, I am Dorothy Adams." The young clerk shook hands with Dorothy very enthusiastically.

"Tiffany Brooks." She pumped with both hands. "Billy has told me so much about you it is an honor to meet you I can't wait to tell my best friend you are actually here!" Tiffany's words came out in a rush without a breath.

"I'm glad I could make your day, Tiffany." Dorothy acknowledged the girl's excitement and felt touched. "May I have my room now?"

"Oh yes certainly! Of course!" Tiffany finished with the transaction and reached for a key in one of the pigeon holes behind the desk. "Your room isn't ready yet so we put you in the Presidential Suite!" Tiffany handed the key to Dorothy with a flourish. "No extra charge, of course."

Dorothy thanked her and went up the stairs with her bags in hand and started to feel the pull of exhaustion. Opening the door to her "Presidential Suite" Dorothy smiled. It was all in blue; blue rugs, light blue walls, pictures with more blue, and the counter in the little ensuite kitchen was blue. The doors to the bathroom and the separate bedroom were also blue. The darkness of the color of the two doors matched the color of the baseboards. What color was the bedspread on the queen sized bed? Blue. What color was the washroom? Blue, including the tub and the toilet.

"*Oh brother.*" Dorothy shrugged. "*All this blue could be a little grating on the nerves after a while. If this is the Presidential Suite, I wonder what the other suites look like.*" Dorothy only unpacked what she had to in order to have a shower and a change of clothes. Her uncertainty about whether she would be welcomed at the Manor by her parents made her reserve this room at the hotel the family owned.

There was no love lost between Dorothy and her father. A stern and demanding father, he was never one given to displays of public affection. *"A child should be seen and not heard."* Was one of her father's favorite sayings. Each of Dorothy's brothers and sisters were assigned tasks at an age her father thought appropriate for. If the task was too huge for the child, their father would tell their mother that *"The child shall grow into his/her responsibilities."* Their father never had the time or the willingness to be in their young lives. Dorothy accepted that truth right from the start. Other children's fathers seemed to take an active role in their children's lives. Often, Dorothy would wish she was someone else's child.

Dorothy's mother, was the exact opposite. She often held the children while they were sick and sang lullabies and sponged their hot little foreheads, while spinning an engaging tale from memory. When their father was tough and stern, their mother was warm and exciting. She had a wisdom in her soul that entranced Dorothy the first she sensed it.

Always able to find the strength to take on whatever happened; Dorothy's mother was the love that held the family together. If it hadn't been for her mother's love, Dorothy would never have made it through the time of her greatest trial. After she left Redwood, Dorothy kept up a string of letters every other day. Many of them were never answered because of her father's wishes, but Dorothy knew her mother loved her unconditionally, and that was enough for her.

CHAPTER TWO

Once Dorothy was finished in her room she went downstairs again to have coffee and a sandwich in the café. Tiffany was not behind the desk when Dorothy went past to the double French doors of the café. The café was small but nicely decorated as a small bistro like eatery. It was close to the dinner rush so Dorothy chose a table for two and she had no sooner seated herself when Tiffany came over with a rush.

"Hi. Remember me?" She asked with her pearly whites flashing in the most engaging smile. Tiffany stood nervously beside the table fidgeting with the buttons on her vest while she waited for Dorothy's reply.

"Of course I do, Tiffany." Dorothy half raised herself and extended her hand in friendship. "Won't you join me?" Tiffany excitedly clasped Dorothy's hand and sat across from her as Dorothy once again settled in to her place. "Tell me, Tiffany, are you working here as well?"

Tiffany's face turned red with embarrassment and she looked down to hide it. "No." she confessed. "I was waiting to see if you would come down for dinner." It isn't all that great to have dinner alone in a strange town." Tiffany's hands became very active as she spoke. Looking at Dorothy, Tiffany continued to explain. "I mean, I know you used to live here and all, but it has changed a lot in the past few years and I thought, I mean, I know I would be lonely, and I guess I just assumed you would feel the same seeing as the town is virtually completely different and all . . ." her voice trailed off as she struggled to explain. Dorothy was touched by the thoughtfulness of the young lady in front of her.

"Tiffany, I would love it if you would join me and yes, it is a little daunting returning to find everything changed. It doesn't even seem to be the same town." Tiffany brightened at her words and Dorothy smiled back at her. "Shall we order? Then you can tell me who's who and what's what." Tiffany nodded and reached for the menu. It took several minutes for the waitress to get to their table and by that time the ladies had decided on their meals and their drinks. Throughout their meals Dorothy found Tiffany to be a thoroughly delightful and engaging conversationalist. She was extremely outgoing and very intelligent. They were just finishing up their meal when an extremely rough looking young man with tattoos, spiked hair, pants below his butt held up with a black leather studded belt, and the most horrible scented cologne Dorothy had ever smelled came walking up to their table. The café had slowly filled while they were eating their meal and the din of the background noise was softly muted in a peaceful soothing sort of way.

"Hey Tiffany. Didn't see you at my party last night. I thought I told you to be there." The youth removed a toothpick from his mouth and dropped it on the table with insolence while Tiffany's face went white.

"Todd, I told you I don't want to see you, talk to you, or smell you. Please leave." Dorothy's anger at the disrespectful way Todd treated Tiffany was tempered by the impressive display of courage Tiffany showed in standing up to the kid. Todd reached out to touch Tiffany's cheek and she turned her head away. The sneer that appeared on his face made Todd look that much uglier.

"Bully's never win, Todd. Didn't your mother teach you any manners?" Dorothy calmly placed her napkin on her plate and stood. She motioned to the waitress who cautiously approached.

"I ain't talking to you, b—h! Remember your place and keep quiet!" His short sentences were punctuated by a leather clad fist with a single finger making stabbing motions to make his point. Dorothy reached out with her left hand and grabbed Todd's wrist. Using the thumb on her right hand, she pressed down on the pressure point in Todd's wrist and he immediately went down on one knee from the pain. Tiffany jumped up in surprise and stepped back. Everyone in the café was watching with rapt attention. Unfortunately the waitress stood rooted to her spot and wouldn't come any closer.

"Now Todd," Dorothy calmly spoke her words as all other sounds stopped. "I want you to apologize to this young lady here for your slovenly manners." Dorothy applied a little more pressure.

"Aaagh! My hand!" Todd almost screamed. "Someone call 911! I want the cops here now!"

A chair scraped back somewhere behind her and Dorothy assumed it had been the police officer that had been sitting behind Dorothy's table.

"Now, Todd. The pain will go away and you will be fine and undamaged as soon as you apologize." Dorothy sounded like a mother disciplining an errant boy.

"F—k you, bitch! Call 911!" His words were directed to Tiffany who started to shake her head.

"No, Todd. The cops are already here. You were the one harassing me and you deserve to be arrested." Tiffany spoke up when everyone else turned their heads away. A hand came down upon Dorothy's shoulder from behind.

"Officer?" Dorothy asked without looking to see who the owner of the heavy hand was.

"Yes Miss Adams? Could you use some help here?" The sound of a warm, deep and exciting male voice came to her ears and made Dorothy want to shiver right down to her boots.

"Chief!" Todd was panting with frustration, rage, and pain. "I have been assaulted and I want to file charges!" He yelled from his kneeling position on the floor.

The man stepped into view and Dorothy was able to see the most exquisite male she had ever seen to date in a uniform. He was tall, over 6 feet. His body was well maintained from his hair right down to his fingernails. That twinge hit Dorothy again as she realized she was instantly attracted to this man with the sandy hair, green eyes, and sexy voice. While she studied his profile, the man reached out to take Todd's wrist out of Dorothy's hands.

"Todd, you haven't apologized to the young lady for your disrespect and harassment." The Chief clasped a pair of handcuffs on the relinquished wrist and pulled Todd to his feet. "And you haven't apologized to the owners of this establishment for disrupting an otherwise peaceful mealtime." The Chief swung Todd's other arm behind his back and closed the cuffs on him.

"I am being abused!" Todd hollered as the Chief began walking him toward the door.

"No, Todd, you're being abusive, not abused." The Chief almost flung the youth through the doors of the restaurant. As the doors closed behind them they heard the Chief's voice once again.

"Todd, you'll never learn. This time you have made a big mistake."

There was a moment when the silence in the café became awkward because no one knew what to do next. Tiffany straightened her chair and sat back down.

"Waitress, could I have a coffee please?" Tiffany smiled sweetly to the waitress whose mouth was still open. Tiffany was carrying on as if the little scene just played out was all in her stride.

"Uhh, yes ma'am." She quickly shuffled away to the coffee station where a fresh pot had just been brewed. Dorothy smiled while placing her elbow on the table and she continued to smile at Tiffany's composure.

Well that was interesting." Tiffany commented with a smile as she looked at Dorothy. Dorothy laughed so hard she almost had tears in her eyes. The mood in the room was instantly transformed back to the light, relaxing atmosphere it had been before the disruption. It seemed everyone needed more coffee, and dessert as well. The hum of a happy little café was evident as the Chief walked back into the room, dusting his hands. He stopped at Dorothy's table and greeted the two ladies.

"Miss Adams, I'm Chief Ethan Barns. It's a pleasure to formerly meet you." His eyes twinkled and reflected his merriment at the absurdity of the situation he had been in just moments before.

"Chief Barns!" Dorothy acknowledged with a hand shake. "Tiffany and I were just talking about you and how you handled the situation in such an efficient manner." Dorothy's eyes held laughter and admiration as well for the perfect specimen of manhood standing in front of her. Perfect for her, that is. Their hands remained in contact just a fraction of a second longer than necessary. "Please, won't you join us?" Dorothy motioned to their table.

"Oh, I'm sorry. I have to get to the office and make out a report. I assume you want to press charges?" The murmur in the room grew quiet again as if awaiting Dorothy's answer.

Dorothy glanced at Tiffany and noticed her discomfiture as she tried to look anywhere but at Dorothy. Dorothy looked back at Chief Wells and nodded.

"Yes I do." Dorothy answered firmly. The Chief drew a business card out of his pocket and placed it on the table.

"This is where you can reach me, my dear. I hope you don't back out." With a nod of his head and placing his hat back on his head he turned and marched out of the doors. Dorothy instantly felt as if the room was barren and cold. It had been so full of only the two of them when they touched, and Dorothy knew she had made the best kind of friend she could ask for.

Tiffany cleared her throat and Dorothy realized she was still looking at the spot where the Chief had gone through the doors. Shaking her head she turned back to face Tiffany.

"Tiffany, what did he mean by that last little comment?" Dorothy quizzed the young lady across from her.

"Well, uh, Todd isn't exactly the nicest person in the whole world. He goes around doing what he wants when he wants and doesn't care what anyone thinks of him. He's a bully who seems to get away with everything he does because people are afraid of him and his friends." Tiffany explained.

Dorothy's chin was in her hand as she leaned forward with a little uneasy smile. "I guess he has his sights on you, does he?" Tiffany lowered her head to hide the fear and nodded.

"But he can't get away with it this time. There were too many people here, and the Chief was here as well." Tiffany's head raised a little with pride and hope as she said this.

"Why does he intimidate so many people? Why do so many people let him get away with it?"

"Because he has some friends who think the same way he does. Disrespect them and he comes down on you like a ton of bricks. He calls it hammering the opposition."

"Tiffany, does he run a gang?" Dorothy knew there were some problems in city but the fact there might be a gang running around really surprised her.

"It's not really a gang, honest. He just likes to run things and make people scared. He likes the power of running with guys like himself."

"Well, sounds like he and his friends would do well in the armed forces." Dorothy finished her coffee and thanked Tiffany for the company and the conversation.

"You mean you're not upset that Todd showed up?" Tiffany asked with surprise. Dorothy reached across the table and touched Tiffany's hands in a gesture of warmth.

"No. How could I be mad at you? It wasn't your fault. That's life and we dealt with it. Right?" Tiffany sat a little taller in her chair and nodded.

"Right, Miss Adams."

"Tiffany, after what we've just been through, I think you can call me Dorothy." Tiffany's smile almost blew Tiffany away.

"Thank you Dorothy. And please, call me Tiffany. Oh wait. You already do." She shook her head at her own silliness and rose to leave as well. Dorothy laughed and said goodnight then paid for the meal and went upstairs to use the phone in her room.

Sitting on the edge of the bed, Dorothy took a deep breath to ease the tension of the moment for what she was about to do. Picking up the phone she called the home number of the Manor and waited anxiously. After four rings, Matt picked up the phone.

"Matt, it's Dorothy." Dorothy breathed a little sigh of relief. The moment of contact she had been dreading was once more delayed.

"Dorothy, hi. Where are you?" Matt's voice seemed to have a little warble in it. Dorothy knew instantly something was wrong.

"I'm at the Inn. What's wrong? What's happened?" Dorothy's voice caught with concern for her family.

"It's Dad. He is not feeling well and the doctor recommends he doesn't see anyone or do anything that will cause him stress. Everyone here has decided that maybe you should stay away for tonight." Matt cleared his voice and Dorothy once again felt the strains of emptiness that seemed to settle on her whenever she had to deal with the attitude of her over protective family. They still viewed her with suspicion over the past.

"Well I realize that the rest of you could be right, but that doesn't mean I can't come to see Mom." There was a silent pause and then Matt released a breath into the phone with resignation.

"Okay, I guess you're right. Could you wait until Dad has settled?" Dorothy's anger at the familiar treatment began to burn slowly from deep inside.

"Of course, we don't want to upset Father now, do we?" The sarcasm wasn't missed by Matt.

"Dorothy, I'm sorry. I know this is hard for you. But we think it is best for everyone concerned, including Mother. Please?" The plea for understanding was met with a quiet pause.

"Okay Matt." Dorothy released a pent up breath. "For Mom's sake, I will wait for another hour before I come over."

"Thanks, sis. Oh, and don't ring the doorbell . . . ."

"I know, it might wake up Dad. I'll knock." Dorothy affirmed her intentions to reassure her brother. He knew she would do anything for their Mother and always would.

Dorothy hung up and ran her hand through her hair. It appeared she was going to have to handle family matters delicately and she wasn't sure she could do it.

"S—t! Kandahar seemed easier than this." She murmured to herself. "Oh well. This gives me time to go down to the station to file my complaint on my way to the Manor." The thought of seeing Chief Barns again motivated Dorothy to grab her jacket and helmet and almost sprint down the stairs.

By the time Dorothy found the address on the card, she was lost and frustrated. So much had changed while she had been away. There were more people, more cars, more houses, more stores, and actually a total of thirty-three street lights where before there were only four way stop signs. The police station had been not too far from the Manor before but now it was way across the city. Pulling into the lot, she parked next to the handicapped spot in front. Entering the outer door, she pushed the buzzer for admittance into the office. An older smaller man in uniform rose from his desk and reached for the buzzer. Walking through the door, Dorothy walked right up to the front counter and spoke to the officer behind the bullet proof glass. Other than the two of them, Dorothy couldn't see anyone else. Disappointment tempered Dorothy's good nature and she almost barked out a command to see the Chief.

The officer was surprised and leaned on his elbows on the front counter with a look of disapproval.

"Now listen, young lady, an attitude like that will get you nowhere." Dorothy saw the look in the officer's blue eyes and knew he was right. Resignedly she nodded and agreed.

"You're right, sir. I'm sorry. It's been a long day and it isn't over yet." Dorothy's apology was met by a nicer look on the officer's face.

"I hear ya, young lady. I hear ya." He nodded in agreement. "Let's start over, shall we?" Dorothy nodded and introduced herself, showing the officer her ID and explaining that she was there to sign a complaint against a fellow named Todd.

"Oh so you're the little spitfire who nabbed Todd Belknap." The officer nodded with glee. "Good for you. We've been after the little bugger for a while now but no one has the guts to sign a complaint."

"You know, that is the second time I've heard that." Dorothy mentioned as she signed the complaint form handed to her through the secure window. "What does that mean?" Then Todd's last name dawned on her and she remembered the run in with Darien Belknap at the gas station earlier. "Oh no!" Dorothy's hand smacked her forehead.

"What's wrong?" The officer questioned her. "Did the Chief get something wrong?"

"No. It's just that I've had run-ins with two Belknaps already and I haven't been here for very long." Dorothy told the officer of her run in with Darien Belknap earlier and the officer nodded.

"Yep! Sounds like Todd's Uncle. Blonde wife, yellow convertible, two boys, and a brick on his shoulder."

"Yeah. That's the man." Dorothy confirmed.

"Sweetheart, you have to watch your back now." The officer shook his head.

"Thank you officer. And by the way," Dorothy called him back to the window.

"Yes?" The officer smiled.

"My name is Dorothy, okay?" The officer waved and pushed the button to release the door.

Back on the bike and retracing the familiar route to the Manor, Dorothy was glad she had thought to put her trailer in Matt's compound.

The streets were deserted and quiet at this time of the night and Dorothy could actually see the stars as they shone so brightly in the night sky. Once again at the top of the loop, Dorothy turned the bike into the access road and stopped. The view was so breathtaking. Sitting at the picnic table placed there for just such an occasion, Dorothy gazed at the mountain and the moon beside it.

This was where she used to sit when she was younger and everyone was pressuring her to fall into line with the family instead of following her own dreams. She would sit for hours, gazing at the mountain and all of its splendor and plan what she wanted her life to be. For Dorothy, the dreams were cast aside though when a car accident she was involved in caused two young people in the backseat to die. Dorothy's boyfriend had been driving but both of them had been ejected from the front seat, and her boyfriend had pointed his finger at Dorothy as the driver. She had only been with him for a couple weeks because she had found he was like a rebel and exciting. That move on her part had hurt her long time boyfriend but as with all youth at that time in their lives, Dorothy was more concerned with her own feelings, wants and needs.

The police charged her with manslaughter and she went to the juvenile court, screaming all the way that she was innocent. Her boyfriend had been the son of the Chief of Police and nothing Dorothy said was heard. Even her father had backed the police because Dorothy felt he didn't have time to listen to Dorothy. While in Juvenile Detention, Dorothy wrote to her mother but her father would never talk to her. He felt his time spent training her to be another one of his yes robots had been wasted. Dorothy turned eighteen and was released. Her record was sealed and she received word from her father that she was not wanted at the Manor. That letter closed off a lot of hurt for Dorothy as she fought to rebuild her life. It felt to her as if a big block of ice had formed inside and couldn't be dislodged. Her family wouldn't talk to her because her father had told them over and over how much of a liar and story teller Dorothy was. How could they not think that way? Every where she turned, Dorothy met with the same attitude. She wasn't angry with her siblings, because she understood that they had been brainwashed enough by society and their own father. They still saw her through their father's eyes. What did make Dorothy angry was her family was all grown up and making their own choices now, so why did they keep seeing the Dorothy of the past? They could see the real Dorothy if they changed their attitudes like she had.

Her brother's Matt and Brent married; Matt to Brenda and Brent to Rosie. Then eventually Dorothy's two younger sisters married as well. Patricia met Mark in high school and Evelyn went away to college and married a pharmacist named Robert. Each of them started their own families and their own businesses with such a single minded purpose, they didn't have time for anything but their families. Dorothy had missed that time in their lives because her father had forbidden contact with Dorothy.

Shaking her head, Dorothy replaced her helmet and sat astride her bike. She had one more person to see before she could sleep tonight; her mother.

The bike glided into the driveway of the Manor almost silently and purred to a stop. The joy of being home washed over Dorothy as she sat for a moment and gazed at the front door. Her mother was behind that door. The kindest and most forgiving person she had ever known. How she had met and married their father amazed Dorothy.

Approaching the door with trepidation for what would greet her, Dorothy hesitated before knocking. At that second, the door flung itself open as if it operated on air. Billy was standing there with a smile and a hug and Dorothy's nervousness disappeared.

"Aunt Dorothy. You're home." Billy's voice was muffled as he clung to her. He released her and Dorothy stepped back to view the living room and the people inside.

Her older brother Brent and his wife and kids, and her sisters Patricia and Evelyn stood in the background with their families. Matt stepped forward and gave her another big bear hug.

"Glad you're home sis. Come in. We have a lot of talking to do." Matt's welcome was the exact opposite of the others as Dorothy surveyed the looks on their faces. She didn't back up or look down. She wasn't going to give them an inch. Looking back at Matt she tapped him on the shoulder like she used to when she wanted to get his attention.

"Actually, Matt. I really only came over tonight to speak with Mom. Is she here?" Dorothy stood tall with pride and anticipation as she turned her back on the hurt behind her. A noise from the door of the kitchen made Dorothy take a sharp breath. As she turned to face her mother who was framed in a glow of light from the kitchen behind her, she felt a pull so strong; then her mother opened her arms. Dorothy glided forward and hugged her mother for the first time in fifteen years. Tears fell from both their eyes as they refused to let go. The love, strength, and warmth that Dorothy felt from her mother's embrace made her feel as if she had finally come home.

Dorothy looked up into her mother's eyes and before she could say anything, the gentle touch of her mother's hand washed over her cheek and soothed the pain in both their souls. Turning her cheek into the hand, Dorothy tried to speak.

"Sshhh! I know sweetheart. I know it all. I am just so blessed to have you home now after all you've been through." The quiet words echoed the emotion in her mother's eyes and Dorothy knew her mother's spirit had been with her through all her suffering. Dorothy nodded and held her mother close once more.

"She's damned lucky she's even here." Came the quiet murmur from Brent's wife. Dorothy turned from her mother's embrace to deal with the comment when her mother spoke.

"Enough! Dorothy is a member of this family. I need her here. I need all of you here. It's time to be a family again." Her Mother's voice was soft but held the ring of steel. She turned back to Dorothy and hugged her again. "Welcome home my girl. I've missed you so much."

CHAPTER THREE

Dorothy sat in the kitchen of the large home with her mother and the rest of the family to have tea and talk about the good times they all shared. Dorothy realized she had a lot of catching up to do. Soon it was time for the children to go to bed and their mothers tucked them in. This gave Dorothy some alone time with her two brothers and her mother. Dorothy sat beside her mother holding her hand while Brent and Matt sat across from them. Matt carried the conversation for the first little while as Brent sat back and seemed to be surveying Dorothy. Dorothy finally couldn't stay quiet any longer. Turning to direct her comment to Brent, she looked him straight in the eyes and smiled.

"So what have you decided about me, Brent? You're so quiet, I think I would like to know." Dorothy sat back and waited for his reply. Brent, who looked the spitting image of their father, tall, dark, and serious, suddenly cracked a smile.

"Would it make a difference to you?" Brent leaned forward with his arms crossed on the table.

Dorothy sat forward as well, mimicking Brent. "No. I'm just curious as to why you are so quiet." There was a slight pause as Brent cocked his head to one side.

"I think that you have finally come home all grown up and changed." His smile was easy and gentle as he continued. "It's good to have you home again, Dottie." Ever since they were little, Brent had called Dorothy by her nickname. He knew it infuriated her as she hated it so much. He even bought her a birthday present one year. It was a nice white blouse with pink dots all over it. Dorothy never wore it. At the mention of her old nick-name Dorothy sat back laughing and shaking her head. Matt and their Mother joined in.

"I haven't heard that name since I left." Dorothy chuckled.

"Well it sure is good to hear you laugh again, even if you still sound like a little hyena." Brent tossed a wadded up napkin across the table. Dorothy held her hands up to ward off the attack.

"Here, here!" Their mother scolded. "There will be no fooling around at my table." The two siblings grinned at each other and sat back in their chairs as their mother poured them some more tea. Even she had a smile on her face.

"When are you going to be moving back into the Manor here?" Matt asked. "We can make room for you somewhere I'm sure. The rest of us have homes to go to. Staying at the Inn could turn out very expensive."

"I don't know Mom." Dorothy looked at her Mother for advice. "What do you think? Would Dad be able to handle it?"

"I don't think it would be a good idea right now." Brent spoke up before their mother could. "Pushing it too soon might cause a bigger gap between the two of you right now. How about staying with one of us for now if your money is tight?" Brent seemed genuinely concerned about the situation and Dorothy silently blessed him for it.

"I hate to say this, Dorothy, but your brother is right." Their mother said. "We want to do this right so that he understands you are home to stay. I will not have you leaving me again." As she said this her hand once more reached for Dorothy's.

"All right, Mom." Dorothy sat forward. "I won't have the need for a room at your houses, though, pushing that button might prove detrimental as well. The girls have to accept me as well before I go putting fuel to the fire. And don't worry, I am not strapped for cash." Dorothy assured the three of them. Rising from her chair, Dorothy said good night to her brothers as they walked her to the door. Her mother stood in the doorway of the kitchen and smiled as she gently waved good night.

Once outside Brent took a deep breath as he walked beside Dorothy to her bike. The stars could be seen so clearly in the dark night sky. Dorothy breathed in as well.

"You don't get air like that in Kandahar." Dorothy observed out loud. "Or Toronto." Brent glanced over at her.

"So how are you doing with that, sis?" Brent questioned. Dorothy looked back at Brent and knew his concern was genuine.

"I'm over it. And I really don't want to go back there." Brent saw the pain in her eyes and put his arm around her shoulder.

"Okay. Just asking, that's all." They reached the bike and Dorothy slipped her helmet on.

"Coming back tomorrow?" Matt asked.

"Yes. As soon as I have slept a thousand years and had a hot bath, I will call you, okay?" Dorothy smiled with her reply.

"Only a thousand?" Brent kidded. "I bet you don't get out of bed before noon. You always had a hard time getting up." Dorothy laughed.

"How much?" She asked.

Really? You want to bet?" Brent thought for a second.

"Yes. I want to bet. Come on! Let's have it!" Dorothy shot back.

"Whoa, my short little sister, let me see what I have in my pocket!" Brent's hand came out of his pocket with two fives and a ten. "How about five bucks?"

"Just five bucks? You have twenty bucks right there." Matt pointed out as he joined them.

"Yeah, but I have to buy formula for the baby." Brent said with a laugh.

"Okay then. Five bucks says I will be up before noon tomorrow." Dorothy knew she would win as she had never slept in past five in the morning since she had been in the forces. "See you tomorrow." She glided off down the driveway and onto the street while the boys watched.

"Did you mean what you said back there in the kitchen?" Matt asked Brent as they stood side by side.

"What, about her growing up? Yeah, she seems to be mature. But after what she's been through in her past, and in Kandahar, I think we should reserve some trust."

"What do you mean by that now?" Matt turned to his brother.

"Matt, you've got to admit, even the strongest of men came back from there either damaged physically or emotionally. Dorothy was damaged before she left. I think we have to watch her close." Even though Matt agreed with Brent he hated to admit it.

"That doesn't hardly seem fair, though, does it?" Matt and Brent turned to walk to the door.

"No, but it's true. If Dorothy needs help with anything, we should be there to give it to her, no matter what." Brent gave a big sigh. Before they opened the door to go in Matt stopped Brent.

"Does that mean you will answer the phone if she calls from now on and not just delete the message from your answering machine?" Matt's chin jutted out a bit with anger.

"What the hell are you talking about?" Brent's confusion showed. "And I don't like the way you said that."

"It has happened, you know." Matt explained. "Either the kids would delete the message, or hear it and not tell me. By the time I got them it was too late." Brent looked down and Matt took that as an acknowledgment. "Both my attitude towards her or my actions are to blame for that and the kids picked up on it. Same with Brenda. So we have to agree from now on, if we are to be a family, we stick together on this."

"I never intended that to happen." Brent looked at Matt with the appeal in his eyes. "And you're right. It won't happen again. Not with anyone in the family."

"That's good enough for me." Matt and Brent shook hands and went inside to the warmth of a fireplace and a family hug.

CHAPTER FOUR

Dorothy pulled into the lot behind the hotel and parked. Taking her helmet with her she stopped at the front desk for her room key and asked for messages. The matronly lady behind the desk looked tough enough to take on the quarter back of an NFL team but her smile was certainly welcome. At the door to her room, Dorothy opened the lock and pushed the door open to survey the room first as she had been taught to do. Inside the place was a shambles, and clothes were all over. A letter had been pushed under the door. Dorothy reached down and picked it up using her gloved hand. Going back down the stairs she went over to the front desk.

"Excuse me. I believe we have a little problem." Dorothy gingerly opened the note and laid it flat upon the counter. It was printed in big block letters with a permanent marker. The letter said: LEAVE TOWN OR DIE. The night clerk backed up and immediately reached for the phone.

"Elva, this is Mabel over at the Inn. We've got a threatening note passed to a guest of ours. Could we have a car sent over?" Mabel was quick and to the point.

"Tell them to bring some technicians. My room is a mess!" Dorothy added.

"Yes, it seems the guest's room was burgled as well." There was a pause while Mabel waited for instructions. "Right! Will do!" She hung up and looked squarely at Dorothy. "The car will be here in moments, but we have to secure the door to your room so no one can go in, and place this little beauty in a safe place." Mabel quickly placed the note into a file folder and picked up the phone again. "Bart, you're needed up front here" she barked. Obviously Bart was used to obeying orders from Mabel for he appeared instantly from a staff door at the end of a corridor that led to the bar.

"What's up?" Bart's gruff voice and huge muscles clad all in black told Dorothy she was talking to a bouncer.

"Someone has entered her room without knocking while she was away and messed it up. Cops are on their way and they want someone to watch the door so no one can go in or out." Mabel's voice conveyed her meaning. Bart nodded and looked at Dorothy.

"Okay, young lady, show me the way." Dorothy was impressed by the attitude of the staff. Obviously they knew exactly what to do in an emergency. When they arrived back at the open door of Dorothy's room, Bart's face registered total dismay.

"Aww, Geese!" Bart exclaimed. "We try so hard to maintain privacy and security for our guests and then this happens. F—k! I sure hope you didn't lose anything valuable! J—s Christ!" Bart stopped and stared at Dorothy. "Sorry for the language, ma'am. It won't happen again, I can assure you." Dorothy smiled her reply.

"It's okay, Bart. I've heard worse than that overseas when I was in the forces." Dorothy turned to look into the room from the doorway. Her clothes were ripped and scattered all over. Glass was smashed into the floor, the television was useless, and even the art on the walls had been slashed. The door to the bedroom was closed but the door to the bathroom was open. On the mirror was another note in red this time. Dorothy couldn't read it all but she did catch the word "kill".

Bart was behind Dorothy and he saw the partial note on the mirror. "Well at least we know someone doesn't like you and it wasn't directed at us." Bart's impartial observation didn't help Dorothy's anger much. Her space had been violated and she was threatened all in one day. And people were telling her it is safer to live in a small city than in Toronto. Not a chance!

"Bart, you're not helping!" Dorothy said wryly. "Not at all."

"Oh, sorry. But at least it gives us a place to start." He said.

"Oh yeah?" Dorothy asked. "Where?"

"In your background. This damage was directed at you, not us. Who have you pissed off since you came to town?" Bart's question had merit to it.

"Hmmm!" Dorothy thought out loud. "There was A Belknap at the service station this afternoon. Darien, I think his name was. And then his nephew Todd while I was having a meal with a friend in the café."

"That little son of a bitch!" Bart leaned back against the wall and crossed his arms. "I wouldn't put it past him or one of his crew to do this." Dorothy leaned against the opposite wall of the hallway in a like manner.

"It couldn't have been Darien?" Dorothy inquired.

"Naw!" Brent shook his head. "Darien is a blow hard and a wife beater; too much of a coward to do something like this."

"So why is Darien still roaming around if everyone knows he is a wife beater?" Dorothy asked Bart.

"'Cause he knows how to cover it up. Plus, his wife would never admit anything is wrong." Bart replied.

"Okay, then, if it was Todd, why the two notes? I think one would have been enough."

"Two notes?" Bart looked at Dorothy in surprise. "You mean there is another one besides this one?" he motions towards the suite and the note on the bathroom mirror.

"The first one is downstairs with Mabel." Dorothy answered. "It said LEAVE TOWN OR DIE in big black permanent marker letters."

"It doesn't sound like a crime of passion that note." Bart's square face wrinkled as he thought. "This room destruction *was* done with a passion." This made Dorothy realize that the note was from a different person than the person who created the chaos in her room. Just then, a couple of uniformed police officers approached from the stairs.

"Thanks, Bart." Dorothy shook hands with Bart and turned to greet the officers. Dead tired as she was, she knew it would be a while before she completed her statement or the police finished their search. Bart's idea that there were two people involved was confirmed by the police. They took their pictures and called Dorothy into the washroom to read the note written in her own lipstick.

"I'M GONNA KILL YOU B—H!" was written in red lipstick all over the mirror.

"Damn, he used my one and only lipstick." Dorothy thought to herself.

"Yep. Sounds like Todd Belknap." The male officer said. "As for the other note, we'll take it to the lab and have it processed. I suggest you stay in a different room tonight and try to straighten things out in the morning."

"Okay officer, whatever you say." Dorothy thanked them both.

"And come down to the office tomorrow and make your statement, okay?" The female cop said.

"Sure." Dorothy nodded.

The cops went down the stairs and Mabel came up carrying a new room key, toilet articles, towels, and an extra pillow.

"Come on, young lady. You look bushed. I've got a new room for you downstairs. It ain't the best, but it's clean and close to the front entrance where I can watch it." She patted Dorothy on the shoulder as she led her back down stairs.

Mabel was right. The room was clean, smaller, had a nicer bed, and Dorothy slept very well. If it hadn't been for the front desk calling to let her know that check out time was 11, Dorothy would have lost her bet with Brent.

CHAPTER FIVE

Dorothy woke up the next morning feeling tired and stressed. A shower and a quick cup of coffee didn't even seem to help. Packing her gear back on her bike, Dorothy took out her cell phone. Her watch told her it was five minutes to twelve and she had a bet to win. Going up to the front desk she called the home number of the Manor and waited. Brent answered the phone and Dorothy could hear the laughter in his voice.

"Good morning Dot. How did you sleep? And how do I know you are up and not just languishing in bed?" Brent asked. Dorothy chuckled at the ribbing.

"Good morning to you, sunshine. I have someone who wants to talk to you." Dorothy handed her phone over to Tiffany who was behind the desk this morning.

"Yes? Hello?" Tiffany had a curious look on her face as she inquired who was on the phone. Dorothy looked on with laughter.

"Yes sir. No Mr. Adams. She was up before eleven. She was even down here having coffee." There was a pause while Tiffany tried to keep a straight face. "No sir. She got up on her own." Tiffany finally handed the phone back to Dorothy.

"Hello Brent. It's Dorothy again." Tiffany could hear Brent's raised voice. Dorothy pointed to the phone and then made a circular motion with her finger by her ear. Tiffany nodded her agreement.

"You know, Brent, you are certifiably crazy, don't you?" Dorothy laughed into the phone. "Say listen, I need to stop at the cop shop and sign a statement so I am not going to make brunch but I will be there by Sunday Dinner. Is it still at 4 pm?"

"What the hell happened this time?" Brent hollered into the phone.

"Brent, it wasn't my fault. Someone broke into my room, trashed the place, and left me a note. I even had one slipped under the door." Dorothy explained. There was a pause and then Brent came back with another question.

"Are you okay? You weren't hurt, were you?"

"No Brent. But it was late and the cops said I could stop by and sign my statement this morning." Dorothy hadn't realized she was holding her breath until she heard Brent's concern about her. It was the acknowledgment she had always needed from her brother.

"Okay, Dot. When you are done, come over for dinner and we will discuss what to do then. Father still isn't feeling well so he won't be able to see you just yet. Sorry sis." The sympathy in Brent's voice came through very clearly and a lump formed in Dorothy's throat.

"I understand, Brent. I'll be there." Dorothy said.

"Hey Dot. If you're late, we'll wait for you." Brent's voice was kind and understanding. Dorothy swallowed around the lump.

"Okay. See you soon." Dorothy hung up and turned to Tiffany to pay her bill with shiny eyes and a smile.

"Are you okay Miss Adams?" Tiffany asked with concern.

Dorothy wiped her eyes with a Kleenex and smiled.

"Of course. Everything is fine."

"I heard about what happened last night and I was shocked. We all were. Is there anything we can do for you?"

"No, I am fine. You helped me win a bet with my brother. Now I'm off to sign the complaint, and then Sunday Dinner at the Manor."

"You won a bet?" Tiffany asked. "Is that what all those questions were for from Mr. Adams?"

"Yes, my dear. He bet me when I left the Manor last night that I wouldn't be able to get up before noon. And if it hadn't been for your kindly call I might have lost." Dorothy smiled across at Tiffany. "So I get to buy you a coffee."

"Okay, Miss Adams. It's a deal." Tiffany laughed.

"By the way, my name is Dorothy. Please use it." Dorothy smiled and waved as she walked out to her bike. Placing her helmet on she smiled at Tiffany's complicity in Brent's loss. He had reacted like the old Brent she knew so long ago. It felt good to be home.

It didn't take long for Dorothy to make it to the police station this time. She parked and went in with her helmet under her arm. This time, the older officer wasn't there. It was that smoking hot piece of manhood called the Chief.

"Good morning, Miss Adams." He greeted Dorothy with a smile. "I hear you had another incident last night." He reached for the top form on the top of a stack in front of him at the reception desk. He rose and came over to the counter. Dorothy felt her stomach drop to her toes with that smile.

"Uh, yeah." She stammered. "Last night, yeah." Dorothy looked down and started to fidget as the Chief's direct stare got to be too much for her. Chief Barns smiled knowingly. He seemed to have that reaction on most women.

"I have your statement all typed up right here. The officers were very thorough last night and they didn't find anything more except a few fingerprints on the mirror, the lipstick, and the note that are unaccounted for. We will need to take your prints to eliminate you, okay?" The information sunk in and Dorothy nodded. The gray haired receptionist was watching the two of them from her desk while trying to look busy.

"I'll need you to come to my office so that I can do that. Is that okay?" The Chief looked at Dorothy again and she gulped. Her brain fog suddenly cleared and Dorothy nodded.

"Okay. Let's do it." She replied. She was finding it very difficult to concentrate on walking with her toes all curled up inside her riding boots. And the scent of his cologne seemed to set a buzz off in her brain.

Dorothy was admitted and led to the desk. While the Chief was doing the prints and handing Dorothy a wipe to clean her fingers, Dorothy started asking questions.

"Last night I was talking to Bart from the Inn and we were of the opinion that there were two people involved with the crime. The one note slipped under the door would have been enough. The one on the mirror, it was more in line with the hatred and anger of the destruction in the room. The paper note seemed completely different. As if written by another person. Cold. Hard." Dorothy began to get nervous after being so open with her thoughts. "What do you think?" Dorothy finished wiping her fingers and reached for a pen to sign her statement.

The Chief paused as if weighing his answer. "It's true. I'm surprised you were so observant. But watching those crime shows on television doesn't make you an expert and I want you to leave the detecting to me and my officers, is that clear?" The stern voice and steely eyes made Dorothy think for a second.

"That's clear. But just so you know, I don't watch television. I watch people and record their human nature in my head. I was in the forces and I was able to read more people than I can list. And when it comes to the safety of my family, I will be as involved as I think I should be. Is *that* clear?" The stubborn tilt of Dorothy's chin and the sparks in her eyes made the Chief smile. She was going to be a spitfire to handle. He almost wished she was a member of the force so he could see her every day.

"That's clear. I have one more suggestion." The Chief said quietly.

"And what's that?" Dorothy asked with no trace of sarcasm.

"I think you should stay away from the Manor." Dorothy's anger was aroused.

"Why?"

"Whoever sent you that note, or broke into your room, is not finished." The Chief punctuated his sentence with a tap on the desk. "In my opinion, that would put way too much stress on your family ties. Bringing that type of problem home could cause you more heat and put your family members in danger. Something you don't need with your family at this point." The honesty and the logic seemed to deflate Dorothy's anger. She let out a deep breath and nodded.

"True. But I won't stop going over to see my family. The family Sunday Dinner is at four this afternoon and I have been invited. I've waited much too long to turn that down." Dorothy's voice shook with emotion as she remembered how much she longed to be sitting at the dinner table with her family instead of on patrol, or behind Juvenile bars. The Chief placed his hand on her shoulder in sympathy.

"You can stay in our VIP house if you would like. Or even remain at the Inn. Now that they have been alerted, I could add an officer to their security if you would like." Dorothy felt the electricity of his touch and shrugged it off before it became too much. Getting involved with someone at this point in her life was not something she had planned on or needed to do.

"I'll stay at the Inn. Bart is a pretty good conversationalist." Dorothy gave a wry little smile. "But I'm not going to miss Sunday Dinner at the Manor." The Chief laughed and reached for the phone as it began to ring.

His face became a stone immediately as he listened to the voice on the phone. He closed his eyes and struggled to keep his face neutral. When he opened his eyes he looked straight at Dorothy and they were cold as ice. It almost made Dorothy shiver.

"We'll be right there." He hung up gently and his hand remained on the phone for a fraction of a second too long.

"What's wrong?" Dorothy was disturbed. Something bad had occurred and she surmised it had to do with her.

"Your father passed away early this morning." The Chief looked right at Dorothy again to judge her reaction.

"Father?" Dorothy's past came tumbling back to rest squarely on her shoulders. The weight of it overwhelmed her for a moment and she looked up with tears in her eyes. "How?" She whispered in pain. "He was supposed to be getting better. I just talked to Brent before I came here and he never said anything was wrong." The shiver caught Dorothy at the base of her spine and went all the way up to her neck. Wrapping her arms around herself she started rocking back and forth in silence with tears streaming down her cheeks. Chief Barns noted the genuine grief.

The Chief's face had relaxed in sympathy as he wrapped his jacket around her as if to ward off the grief and the cold.

"We're needed over at the Manor, Miss Adams. You can ride with me." He reached to take her elbow to guide her back through the door as he tried to stifle an impulse to take her in his arms and hold her until the hurt was gone. An officer came up from the back when buzzed in by the Chief. They made their way outside to the car.

"In the front or the back?" Dorothy's lifeless tone of voice still had plenty of fight left in it.

"In the front, Miss Adams. Always in the front." The Chief said quietly as he settled her in the front seat passenger side.

On the way to the Manor in the car they were both silent and Dorothy took that time to go back in her mind and remember when things were better. The family would go to the lake and play on the public beach while their parents would look on. Their father was always at a distance and reading some manual or important piece of literature. He never wore shorts or a t-shirt. The closest he came to casual was a shirt, tie, and slacks. Their mother on the other hand knew how to play in the sand. She taught them how to build sand castles, and fight battles against enemy hordes. If the boys started getting rough she would scold them and make them take care of their sisters. She was always there to sooth a battered knee or the loser in 'King of the Castle".

Now Dorothy realized she would never be able to make things better between her father and herself. Her mother seemed so wrapped up in their father and loved him deeply. Dorothy told herself that now she would have to help her mother the best she could. She was determined that her other family members would not chase her away. What's done was done and there was no use worrying about it. Their mother needed them just as they needed her when they were growing up.

The Chief's car pulled up to the front steps just as it started to rain. Police officers seemed to scatter to find rain gear. Standing at the front door, Dorothy was reluctant to knock, and the Chief knew it.

"It's okay, Miss Adams. Your family is here." He said quietly.

"*He really doesn't know my family the way I know my family.*" She said to herself.

Dorothy used the knocker on the huge wooden door and it opened almost immediately. There, standing on the doorstep was her mother. Dorothy opened her arms and stepped inside to her mother. She held her as the Chief followed Dorothy in and closed the door. Several steps behind was the rest of the family with grief stricken faces and tears held in check. Dorothy held her mother at arm's length.

"It's okay, mom. We're all here for you. We always will be." Dorothy choked back her tears. They had to make room for the gurney the medics were bringing down the stairs. It was draped with a sheet out of respect for the family. A body bag would have been tasteless. As they passed, an officer pulled the Chief to the side and whispered to him. Dorothy turned to face her mother and the rest of her family.

"What happened?" Dorothy asked as she choked over the lump in her throat. "I thought he was getting better?" Her mother hugged her once more.

"Oh sweetheart, I am so sorry you and your father didn't get to talk with each other. You needed closure between you." Her mother's tears ran unchecked down her delicate features. The white hair that complimented her face seemed to be ruffled and reckless compared to her usually immaculate do.

"Mother, don't you know there has been closure? I came to terms with it a long time ago." Dorothy placed a comforting arm around her mother's shoulders. "I'm just worried that Dad didn't have the same feelings I did. It's over and in the past. I would have liked to tell him that."

Matt stepped forward and hugged Dorothy. "He knew it, sis. I really believe he knew it." The rest of the family moved forward and they started talking at once. Forgotten from the moment they walked in the door, the Chief chose this moment to make himself known.

"Excuse me, folks. I will need to speak with you. Can we all go into the room and have a seat?" The Chief motioned to the living room or the "parlor" as it used to be called.

When everyone was seated the Chief cleared his throat and started to fidget with his tie. Dorothy began to get a bad feeling about what he was going to say next.

"Apparently we have a slight problem. The officer who happened to be first responder noticed something wrong and called me. Now I have to inform you we will need to take statements of your whereabouts last night until Mr. Adams was found this morning. I hate to do this when you are in mourning but it has got to be done."

"What do you mean?" Matt asked in confusion. "He died in his sleep, didn't he?"

"Yes, he certainly died in his sleep. But our preliminary findings at this time tell us this was not a natural death." A collective gasp was heard from the room. Dorothy's mother almost fainted and Matt and Brent caught her. They sat her on the couch and Matt's wife Brenda ran for a glass of water. Dorothy hovered in the background as the shock made her immobile.

"What do you mean? What preliminary findings? What's going on here, Chief? I want to know." Dorothy demanded.

"As I said, our findings are preliminary and this makes it an ongoing investigation. I cannot tell you any more than that until the findings are confirmed. Until then, I will need to know where each of you were from the time your father was put to bed until he was found this morning." The stunned looks were directed at the Chief. "I will have several more of my men come in to help with this and I don't want you talking to anyone outside the family."

He turned to Dorothy and looked down at her with sympathy. "May I start with you first?" Dorothy nodded and the Chief took her into her father's kitchen so they could talk.

They passed the office door which was open and papers were strewn all over the floor, file drawers were pulled out, and the desk top was in a shambles.

"What the hell is this?" Dorothy paused at the door without going in.

"We should go to the kitchen to talk. I did want to see your reaction to the mess in the study." The Chief said as Dorothy led the way to the kitchen.

"All right, you've seen my reaction. What does that tell you?" Dorothy asked as they sat at the huge table in the kitchen. The cook placed a cup of coffee and cream and sugar on the table in front of them and turned to go back to the stove.

"Thank you, Maria." Dorothy acknowledged the cook who turned to look at Dorothy with tears in her eyes. "Oh my Maria." Dorothy stood and gave Maria a hug. "I'm so sorry we had to meet again this way after all these years."

"I am sorry too Dot. I was hoping you would come home after being overseas but your father wouldn't have liked it."

"I know. But it's okay. Don't worry about it. I'm okay with it." Dorothy gave Maria another little hug and returned to the table.

"First of all I want to ask you about where you were last night." Dorothy gave the Chief a description of her travels the night before and he nodded. "Okay, this alibi should be easy to verify. Now tell me what Maria meant. Why wouldn't your father have liked you coming home?" Dorothy paused and closed her eyes. The way the Chief handled the following information could ruin Dorothy's future in Redwood. She started with the accident, the subsequent deaths and charges, she even told the Chief of her hurt and emotional turmoil when her father seemed to believe her ex-boyfriend over her. The subsequent verdict and the Juvenile Home followed. Dorothy left nothing out. She told the Chief of her years in the military and trips to Kandahar. She told him about hearing from Matt that it wasn't safe to come home yet and how she created her own world in Toronto and started a business of her own. Then she told the Chief how she sold out her shares in the business and came home when Matt called. She told him of the disapproval of her father in everything she did. During her treatment for PTSD she was able to come to terms with it and put it in the past where it belonged. As she talked, the Chief nodded and wrote as fast as he could. Finally, when Dorothy finished, the Chief looked up and asked her a question she had been dreading.

"You have been having an awful lot of trouble since you came home. Have you made any enemies who might want to see you suffer?"

"You might want to look at Todd and Darien Belknap. But I can't think of anyone who would have known me back then who would be around now except my family and I know none of them did what you're thinking." Dorothy's tone was flat and a little angry.

"Take it easy, Miss Adams. I had to ask. Now, in your opinion, did the event from your past have any bearing on your father's death?" Dorothy was outraged.

"No." she struggled to keep her anger in check. "Whoever did this had nothing to do with me. I've been away for fifteen years."

"Okay." The Chief nodded. "Who do you think would have searched the den?" Dorothy paused. His meaning sank in and she looked up sharply.

"You think it was someone from in the house who ransacked the office?" Dorothy asked. "Why would they do that? There is nothing valuable in the den to be stolen."

"What about the safe?" The Chief asked.

"What safe? The only safe I know of is the one in the master bedroom under the floor in the closet. Father figured we didn't know about it as children but no one else knew except family. So if it was one of us, we would have ransacked the bedroom."

"So if someone ransacked the den, then they did not know there wasn't a safe, correct?" The Chief asked.

"Correct." Dorothy verified.

"Then how come there was no sign of break and enter on the study door." The Chief asked.

"We never lock that door except when father went in there." Dorothy answered. Again the Chief nodded.

"One last question. I know you have a cook, but don't you also have a housekeeper?"

"Yes, but I have no idea where she is. Sunday is her day off. Or at least it used to be. I've been gone for 15 years and have never met her."

"Okay, then. I am going to ask you to remain here at the house until all the statements have been taken." He didn't meet Dorothy's eyes and she knew, deep in her heart, that he didn't believe her story about the accident and not being the driver.

"Not a problem. I'll help Maria here. I think she could use a hand." Dorothy got up and turned her back on the Chief before he could see the hurt in her eyes. And it was suddenly so very important to Dorothy that this man believe her.

CHAPTER SIX

The Chief made sure all the officers involved in the investigation reported to him with any findings and then he gave his sympathies to Mrs. Adams. He wanted to get back to the office and look up the file on Dorothy Adams. Despite his attraction to her something did not sit right with him about the way she described her previous charges and the investigation into them. He was loath to admit that an officer of the law would actually ramrod an investigation of an innocent person the way Dorothy described it.

Entering the building he went straight to his office. He booted up his computer and tried to pull up the file on Dorothy Adams. He found the file was sealed because of her age and he went straight to the office receptionist.

"Elva, I need your help with a file. Could you please come in here?" He requested. Elva picked up her steno pad and hurried into the office, closing the door behind her.

"I have been trying to get into the file that has been sealed but I am unable to." The Chief turned the monitor towards Elva so she could see. She wrote the name and the number of the file on her pad and then she realized who it was the Chief was inquiring about.

"You know, Chief, you may not get that file unsealed." Elva mentioned as she finished writing down the information.

"Why not?" the Chief asked.

"It was a difficult case for the Chief back then. His son was involved somehow and everyone on the force seemed pretty upset. I was surprised the judge was as lenient as he was." Elva's loyalty was obviously with the former Chief but she did give Chief Barns a clue as to how the investigation could have gone. Knowing he had to treat Elva with kid gloves he looked right at her.

"I understand that, Elva, but I need to find some of the details. This death over at the Manor seems a little strange to me and I want to see if there isn't a motive somewhere in that file." He deliberately didn't say a motive for who and let Elva believe what she liked so he could get into the file. Elva nodded her head in agreement.

"I see. Okay, I will contact my buddy over in records and you should have it shortly." Elva smiled and left the office.

Chief Ethan Barns mentally let out a big sigh. *"I think I am going to have to tread lightly on this one. No suppositions or erroneous decisions. I will have to go through the file and read it very carefully. Investigating a former convicted offender is one thing, but if word gets out a cop is investigating a cop, that thin blue wall becomes impenetrable."*

Elva was true to her word. She walked back into the Chief's office with the file and placed it on the desk with a smile. It was in a file box which she placed directly in the middle of the desk.

"I was pretty sure you needed this as soon as possible. It's all the original files and evidence. Even the trial transcript." Chief Barns was dumbfounded as he looked back up at Elva.

"Thank you Elva! Remind me to give you a nice bonus in your next pay cheque." Elva, knowing that would never happen, just smiled and went back to her desk.

"*Interesting. Very interesting.*" For the next several hours, Chief Barns read through the file on Dorothy's case. Dorothy claimed her innocence even back then. Quite loudly, actually. He put the transcript to the side and looked through the evidence. All the measurements, the pictures of the mangled wreck, the tire tracks, etc. While going through the pictures a second time, he noticed something strange in the front car section. Getting out his magnifying glass, he took a closer look. The seat seemed to be in a position that was for someone with very long legs. A tall person over six feet, perhaps. Chief Barns sat up and shook his head.

"Well, well. What have we here?" The Chief said out loud to himself. "I wonder how anyone could have missed this." Digging through the file he took out the sheet on Dorothy Adams and read it over. Shaking his head he searched for the sheet on the other person who emerged alive and unscathed. Whistling through his teeth he laid it back in the file.

"I guess I am going to have to talk to this little lying prick and find out what he has to say for himself. Son of the Chief or no son of the Chief, he is now a suspect in something bigger." Chief Barns also knew he couldn't approach any of the investigating officers without causing more problems. None of them would cooperate once they got wind of this whole mess. The phone on his desk rang as he sat thinking. All the police procedures had been by the book, so why was this one vital piece of evidence missed? He reached for the button on the intercom.

"Yes, Elva?" He answered.

"It's your Detective over at the Manor." Elva's voice informed the chief.

"Put him on." The Chief sat back with his boots on the edge of his desk. "Harmon, what's up?"

"Well, we've pretty well wrapped up everything we can do here except one thing."

"What's that?"

"It seems the housekeeper cannot be located. It's her day off and she may not have heard the news so we left word for the family to contact us as soon as they hear from her."

"Great! When you get back to the office, I want you to give me backgrounds on every member of the family, alive or dead. And the housekeeper and the cook as well."

"Aah, Chief, I was hoping to go home and have a hot meal tonight." Phil Harmon said. "I can stay and rack up some more OT if you want." The Chief looked at his watch and realized it was dinner time.

"Naw, that's okay. Just make sure your notes and reports are on my desk in the morning and you do those checks first thing in the morning as well."

"Okay, Chief. It'll be done. See you tomorrow."

Chief Barns hung up and slowly placed his papers back into the file box. Placing it under his desk he turned out the light and locked the door. Saying good night to the officers on night shift he left the building out the back door. His cruiser was parked next to the back door and he climbed in, closed the door, and thought for a few moments.

"This job has certainly gotten a little more exciting than I counted on." He thought to himself. *"Oh well. It's time to go home and feed the cat."*

His existence in his little apartment had been solitary since the day he had moved in. Coming to Redwood from Ontario meant leaving his old life and all the hurts from his former relationship. It had been doomed from the start of his police career and Ethan had never seemed to recover from that loss. Trusting someone was not automatic for him, as it used to be. Still, the memory of a certain little fiery woman named Dorothy seemed to awaken something inside him that had been missing for quite a long time. Ethan could see Dorothy's smile swimming in the back of his mind and knew it was time to start living again. Even his cat would agree.

CHAPTER SEVEN

Dorothy woke up the next morning still in her room at the Inn. The phone was ringing shrilly by her ear and the sun was streaming in through the gap in the curtains. Answering the phone was the only way to stop that noise.

"Hello?" Dorothy said

"Hello, Dorothy. It's me, Patricia." Her sister's voice was hesitant as if she was nervous. "How are you doing this morning?"

"I'm fine, Pat." Dorothy's surprise was evident in her voice as she answered Pat's inquiry. "What is everyone at the Manor up to?"

"Actually we were wondering if you would join us for a late breakfast." Pat answered. "We would like to talk to you about some things." Now Dorothy knew why Pat had been the one to call. She was extending an olive branch after 15 years of silence. How could Dorothy refuse?

"What time is breakfast?" Dorothy mumbled into the phone. "And by the way, what time is it now?"

"Well, breakfast is at 9 and it is 7 right now." Pat's eager voice rushed on before Dorothy could change her mind.

"Oh! That's why I was still sleeping. I thought it was closer to noon and I'm still tired." Dorothy laughed a little. "Of course I will be there, Pat. I would love to have breakfast with everyone."

"Oh, that's just great, Dorothy. We look forward to seeing you. Sorry I woke you but we wanted to get in touch with you before you made other plans." Pat said quickly.

"That's fine. I will be there with bells on." Dorothy smiled into the phone. "See you soon." Dorothy hung up and tried to wake herself up by yawning and stretching then decided the only thing that would help was a nice hot shower.

Once she was dressed and refreshed, Dorothy went over to the curtains and pulled them open. It was going to be a beautiful day. The sun was shining, there was a soft cool breeze to help cool things off, and the air was so clean and clear. "*It's too bad we have to discuss our father's funeral on a day like today.*" Dorothy thought to herself. Straightening her room a little she put a Do Not Disturb sign on the door knob and went down the stairs to the front desk with her helmet under her arm. Tiffany was behind the desk again with a smile on her beautiful youthful face.

"Hi Tiffany." Dorothy called out as she put her key on the desk. Tiffany scooped it up and smiled and waved then went back to helping the guests in front of her.

Once on her bike, Dorothy decided to go through the loop again for sentimental reasons. She went slow and careful and watched the traffic carefully for Todd Belknap or Darien Belknap. Dorothy completed her ritual and turned her bike towards the Manor. It wasn't long and she pulled up the curving driveway. Dorothy was hesitant to go inside on a day like today but she knew it had to be done.

The door opened before she even made it to the top step. Patricia was standing there waiting for her.

"Good morning again!" Pat gave Dorothy a huge hug and a surprised Dorothy was ushered into the foyer. Pat took Dorothy's leather jacket and hung it up on the coat rack. Dorothy placed her helmet on the floor beside her boots and they went in the direction of the living room. Dorothy could smell the breakfast cooking as Maria put the finishing touches on it. When the two women walked into the room side by side, Dorothy's mother rose from the couch on one side of the fireplace and stood in awe of seeing two of her daughters standing side by side for the first time in years. She raised her hands to her lips and threw a kiss to the both of them.

"Good morning mother." Dorothy gave her mother a warm embrace and kissed her on the cheek.

"Now that my whole family is here, we can go in." Temperance Rose led her children into the dining room. Matt had taken her arm and led her to the spot at the head of the table where their father used to sit.

"It's your spot now, mother." Matt kindly explained.

"I know it is, Matthew. But I don't think I can sit in his chair just yet." She looked up into her son's blue eyes with tears in her own. "Humor me on this for a while, please." Matt nodded and led her to the spot to the right. Everyone else took a seat around the large table, leaving the one at the head of the table empty for now.

Dorothy looked around and didn't see any of the children at the table and inquired where they were.

"Billy is keeping them busy in the back yard for now." Temperance explained. "We need some privacy to talk through some very important things." Dorothy nodded and sat. The family served themselves from the hot buffet one at a time and tucked themselves into a delicious meal of sausages, scrambled eggs, fresh melons, toast, and pancakes for those who wanted them. After the plates were cleared and coffee was distributed all around, they became silent once again, waiting for their mother to begin. Everyone seemed to have little smiles on their faces and Dorothy began to wonder what they were up to.

"Dorothy, my dear, we wanted you here today to try and convince you to move back into your old room." Her voice was full of love for her oldest daughter. "It's been too long since you were here last. You belong here, with the family."

Dorothy's look of surprise was met all around the table with smiles of welcome. Matt laughed and patted his sister on her back.

"You can close your mouth now." He said. Laughter and twitters could be heard all around the table from the others. It quieted again while they waited for her answer. Taking a deep breath Dorothy glanced around the table.

"What made you guys decide this and when?" Dorothy asked. "Our history isn't one of family harmony." She also knew Ethan Barns was not going to approve.

"We're going to change that, Dorothy." Said Patricia from her corner seat.

"Yes." Even Evelyn's usually cold stare had warmed with compassion. "It's time we started over and became a real family." Dorothy's face started to form a little smile. She glanced at Matt first, then Brent, Brenda, and Rosie. Mark and Robert, the husbands of Patricia and Evelyn all had the same smile and were nodding their heads in compliance.

"Well," Dorothy looked back at her mother and expelled a breath. "I guess if you guys are willing to extend an olive branch, who am I to ignore it." There were little tears in Dorothy's eyes as she cleared her throat. "It looks like I've come home."

"For good!" Temperance raised her cup and everyone did the same.

"For good!" The cheer rose from the table.

"Now, since we have a missing housekeeper, we will have to enlist your help to clean your old room and help out around the house for a little while." Temperance said.

Dorothy nodded. "Of course. Is there anything else you want to talk about?" They talked about everything from the missing housekeeper to who would be the pall bearers at the funeral.

"I've called Pastor Bob Wingate from the Lutheran Church to do the ceremony and the Centennial Memorial Funeral Home will make all the arrangements. Your father prepaid for our funeral expenses so there isn't much to do but wait for the coroner to release your father to us."

"Has the Chief said anything about that or the missing housekeeper?" Dorothy asked out of curiosity.

"No." Brent chimed in. "I called his office late last night and he asked us to be patient. But the housekeeper was, what's her name mother?" Brent asked.

"Therese." Was her answer.

"Right. Therese is still missing. All of our alibis cleared us so now we just have to wait for them to find her." Brent explained.

"Does he think she did it?" Dorothy asked again. Then she noticed her mother's drawn face and felt ashamed of herself for discussing this topic in front of her. "I'm sorry, mother. Never mind."

"That's quite all right, Dorothy. We all have to face unpleasant things in our life. This is the time for me to start clearing the air. Even if we don't like the answers, they must be found." Temperance rose and went to stand beside Dorothy's chair. Dorothy stood and hugged her mother again. "I'm glad you are home, my dear. For now, I must lay down for a rest." She left the room moving with a quiet grace that touched Dorothy's heart.

The rest of the family rose and set to clearing the table and doing the dishes. If Maria, the cook, was surprised to have all this help in her kitchen, she didn't show it. The smiles and laughter made everyone's lives a little lighter. Slowly the kitchen work was completed and they all moved as one to the stairs.

"Do you ladies need help with the bedrooms?" Matt asked in an innocent voice. Brenda looked at Matt with narrowed eyes and a little smile on her face.

"Why?" She asked.

"Well, the guys and I thought we would go and clean the library. You know, do some dusting." Matt tried to keep the smile from his face but failed.

"You mean you want to dust the pool table?" Brenda asked with a knowing smile.

"Yes, Yeah. Of course. We'll dust the pool table." All the men nodded and the women laughed, shooing them on with a wave of their hands. The women went up the stairs to Dorothy's old room. Opening the door, they coughed and waved their hands over their faces. The dust was thick over everything.

"I thought mom said the housekeeper cleaned this room once a week like she did all the other rooms." Evelyn looked confused.

"She did say that." Rosie answered. "I heard her say that."

"Well obviously she was getting paid to do something she didn't." Brenda quipped. "Well, let's get to work." Dorothy was touched that her room had been kept unchanged all these years as if their mother was just waiting for her to come home and move in. The yellow patchwork quilt that was slightly tattered from use was still on her single bed with little white night stands on both sides of the bed. The closet was along the wall at the end of the bed. A large window with a built in bench beneath it had afforded Dorothy the luxury of sitting there at night, watching the stars and dreaming of a future she had looked forward to; a future she had lost after one bad decision. Shaking her head, she dug in right alongside the others and it wasn't long before they had dusted, beat the rug, vacuumed, washed the walls, and cleaned the bed clothes and blankets.

"Oh my!" Brenda stood with her hands on the small of her back. "I think it is time for a break. What do you girls think?" They all nodded and went back down the stairs in search of a cup of tea and some lunch.

Several of the children stood up from in front of the television and ran to their mothers. Hugs and smiles as introductions were made to their Aunty Dorothy for the first time.

"Let's go and see if Maria needs some help in the kitchen for lunch." Evelyn said. The ladies all trooped into the kitchen with hairs sticking out from their severe pulled back hairstyles, dust all over their faces, and their quiet laughter making the house seem lived in for the first time in a very long time. For Maria, though, it was a bit of a shock.

"You five girls get out of here and go clean up. Lunch will be ready soon. Go on! Get!" Maria shooed the ladies out into the hall to go and clean up. One by one they all cleaned up and filed back into the living room to spend some time with the children and their husbands. Everyone looked up when their mother came into the room.

"Hello mother." Came the chorus from all her children. Temperance stood there and surveyed her family with pride.

"It feels so good to hear all of you say that." Several children ran to her and scrambled to be the first one picked up. "Let's all go in for lunch, shall we?" She said as she picked up the littlest one. The children were all placed around the table with their parents and it was a noisy, happy lunch.

Just as they were finishing, the phone rang and Billy stood to go answer it in the hall. He came back in after several moments and motioned to Dorothy.

"It's for you, Aunt Dorothy." He said as he sat. "It's the Chief."

Dorothy hesitated to stand and most of the adults became quiet and glanced at Dorothy. Out in the hall Dorothy answered the phone on the stand.

"Dorothy here."

"There you are. I thought you were still residing at the Inn for now." The Chief questioned her.

"I am having lunch with my family right now. Can I help you with anything?" Dorothy's voice sounded her displeasure at the interruption.

"Actually I was wondering if you would come down to the station and talk with me. I have some questions for you about your past." Dorothy's happiness at being welcomed back into the family a few moments earlier was dashed at his words.

"All right. When would you like me to be there?" Dorothy asked.

"How about in an hour." The Chief answered.

"I'll be there." Dorothy hung up the phone and went back into the dining room to her place at the table. The children continued to chatter on as the parents waited to see what Dorothy had to say.

"Apparently, the Chief has some more questions about something and wants me down there in an hour. I figured I could round up my belongings after wards and bring them back here. How does that sound?" Dorothy tried to make light of the situation as she spread the napkin over her lap again.

"Sounds interesting." Matt said.

"Need some company?" Brent asked.

"No, I'll be fine, guys. Really." Dorothy said.

"Then why does your face look like a brick dropped on your head just now?" Robert, Evelyn's husband asked.

Dorothy looked up and paused. Laughing at the concern on their faces she smiled.

"You guys could always read me when I wasn't in a good mood." She left it at that and they finished their meal.

CHAPTER EIGHT

Dorothy walked into the police station with a sense of foreboding and went straight to the front desk. She asked for the Chief, told the officer she was expected, and was shown in to the Chief's office.

"Good afternoon, Chief Barns." Dorothy shook the Chief's hand as he stood up to greet her.

"I am glad you came down here, Miss Adams. It makes our conversation a little easier to handle." He motioned for Dorothy to sit in the chair across from the desk. Dorothy noticed the door was closed and she looked at the Chief as he began to fidget in his chair.

"What would you like to talk about, Chief?" Dorothy came right to the point to make it easier for the Chief to form his words.

"Well, I'll come right out with it." Chief Barns began to lean back in his chair. "I went through your old file because I simply didn't believe the facts as you told them to me." Dorothy's face went hard and blank. The Chief continued. "It's one thing to claim innocence and another to point a finger at a member of the law and cry foul. So I went through this entire file and went over all the evidence." He looked straight at Dorothy with a face of stone. Dorothy could not read his profile and she didn't want to.

"*He doesn't believe me.*" She thought to herself. "*If he doesn't believe me, I could be in a big pile of excrement.*" Chief Barns paused and then his stare seemed to soften.

"I found a discrepancy in one of the photographs of the crime scene." He took one of the photos out of the file and put it in front of Dorothy. She carefully reached out to take the photo, afraid of what she would find.

"Do you recognize that picture?" Chief Barns asked.

"No," Dorothy shook her head. "I wasn't allowed to see any of the evidence."

"Why not?" came the obvious question.

"My father forbade it. The Chief back then didn't think I was capable of understanding what happened. And I really didn't want to see pictures of my dead friends." The anger lashed out at the Chief stronger than Dorothy had intended.

Ethan Barns as the Chief of Police, wondered how a mistake like this could have happened back then. He realized that back when this all happened, procedures were different because some scientific methods didn't exist back then like they did now. As well as small town beliefs were not as open and understanding as they were now.

Ethan Barns, widowed bachelor and human being, stared at the curve of Dorothy's jaw line and felt a familiar tug in his gut. Mentally shaking himself, he cleared his throat.

"If you will take a close look at the positioning of the front driver's seat, I want you to tell me what you see." Dorothy stared at the picture but couldn't fathom what the Chief was getting at.

"I don't understand. What is it you want me to see?" Dorothy asked.

"How tall would you say a person would have to be in order to sit comfortably in that driver's seat?" the Chief asked.

"I don't know." Dorothy answered. Then suddenly she sat up as the importance of the answer hit home in her mind. "I was only five foot two back then. My boyfriend was close to six feet. He would have to have adjusted the seat to fit his frame." The excitement of the find gave Dorothy hope. Somebody was starting to believe her. This thought made Dorothy begin to shake.

"Now I don't want you to get your hopes up. But I have been quietly digging into this file, interviewing officers who were there, and they all point to you as being the driver." The Chief's voice was quiet when he talked because he knew the impact the news would have on a 30 year old who had been saying she was innocent for the past 15 years.

"Of course they would say that." Dorothy's stubborn chin stuck out a mile long. "They would agree with whatever the Chief told them to." There was a short pause while Chief Barns evaluated Dorothy's answer.

"I have been told that the last Chief was an officer that earned the respect of his men, was fair and open minded, and took care of victims above and beyond the scope of his job." Dorothy sat back in angry silence.

"Being fair minded myself, when I see an investigation ramroded through the courts without taking into account all of the facts, I do get angry." Dorothy sat up a little straighter when she heard those words.

Looking him straight in the face she could see he was being truthful and not lying to her. "However, that is not the case here. One vital fact had been missed because of crime scene procedures and techniques that were unavailable to us back then. Add that to the fact you were underage and your father never allowed you to stand up for yourself, I came to the conclusion that the police did the best they could with what they had to work with. A miscarriage of justice happened with no one being at fault."

"You mean that?" Dorothy was stunned and leaned forward.

"I do." Chief Barns sat forward and leaned with his arms on the desk. "You have to remember, the Chief back then had to deal with the fact that his son was involved with two deaths resulting from the accident. He recused himself from the investigation. There could have been a miscommunication between the lead detective and the district attorney, or between your father and the district attorney, but ultimately, you had no choice but to accept your responsibility for your part in the debacle, whether you liked it or not."

"So what do we do now?" Dorothy asked.

"Well for one thing, any investigation I do has to be done quietly and carefully. But I do know, and I want you to hear this," Chief Barns finger tapped the file lying open on his desk. "Every single thing Chief Masters did was by the book with the evidence handed to him. He believed in it and your guilt. There were several indescrepancies, information that was missed, not on purpose, but by accident. Back then, evidence was viewed differently than it is today. And I want you to know, divulging the truth right now, could seriously hamper my investigation." Dorothy's anger flared again.

"You mean you just want to sweep it under the rug, right? Will that make life easier for you?" Dorothy stood and pushed back her chair in an effort to leave.

"Sit down!" Came the stern command. Dorothy paused and then sat again.

"All right. I'm still here." She said as she sat.

"Somebody out there killed your father. I think it has something to do with your past and the accident someone *thinks* you caused." The statement made Dorothy pause in her thoughts.

"You think someone deliberately murdered my father? Because of something they think I did?" Dorothy asked. "How did you come to that decision?"

"The little crime spree that has been happening between you and Todd Belknap seems to have covered up a secondary threat that we may have overlooked. Someone who penned that note tucked under you hotel room door wants to do damage to you or your loved ones." Dorothy nodded.

"We have a missing housekeeper. Her identity begins from the moment she came to Redwood and we can't find any background before that." Chief Barns said. He sat back with a sigh. "And everyone in the house has an alibi, including you. They have all been verified. Except for the housekeeper whose name is Therese Billings. She has simply vanished from the face of the earth. We are still doing some digging and hopefully the fingerprints we took from the odd personal items will come back with her real name. If she has never been in trouble before, I sincerely doubt it. Until we find her, though, I need you to remain silent for me. That may be the only way to flush her out of hiding if she's still alive." Dorothy sat back nodding in compliance.

Relief washed through Dorothy. Finally, someone believed her beyond all reasonable doubt. Tears formed in her eyes and threatened to spill down her cheeks but Dorothy refused to let them fall. Taking a deep breath she looked back at the Chief and nodded.

"I know this has been difficult for you but you made it through and you are stronger than most of the men in my employ. Your character is beyond reproach for the way you reacted to what has happened to you. When you had an opportunity to get revenge, you chose to let it go and live your own life. Now I need you to act as if everything is still the same in public. If you want to tell your mother, you may do so, but keep it to yourselves; I don't want it leaking out before we catch this person." Dorothy nodded in silence again.

"Okay, Chief. Whatever you say." Dorothy said. "What else can I do to help?"

"I want you to go through the housekeeper's room and her personal things. I need to know anything that may be a clue to her past. Talk to your mother and ask her questions, see if she remembers anything else about her. If I were to do that, the word would be out we are investigating her and I don't want that right now."

"Sure, I can do that." Dorothy nodded. "What about my family. Is there any danger to them?"

"I don't know. But I am not going to doubt that. So bearing in mind your background in security, you could keep an eye out. Watch for anything that could be unusual."

"All right. Do I call you if I find anything?" Dorothy asked.

"Yes. Just call the front desk and the receptionist will get word to me. Tell her you have the file I needed. I'll know what you mean." The two of them rose from their chairs and shook hands. Ethan looked into Dorothy's warm moist eyes and felt a tug. He fought the desire to engulf her in his arms and keep her safe. Instead he stepped back and smiled.

"There is another thing you can do for me." Chief Barns said as they approached the door to the office.

"What's that?" Dorothy asked.

"That bike of yours is a big target to anyone looking to harm you. Park it and get a car. Nothing flashy. I think you can afford it."

"What do you mean? Was that a parting shot?" Dorothy smiled. She had felt the same tug. Surprisingly to Dorothy, it felt very good.

"No. I did my background check on you as well. That's my job. The money you got from the sale of your high end security business in Toronto is definitely enough for a new car." The smile on his face was genuine as he let Dorothy back into the reception area of the office. They were both smiling when Dorothy left.

"*Oh yeah!*" Chief Barns thought to himself. "*I am definitely going to enjoy getting to know her a little better when this is all over.*"

CHAPTER NINE

The sun seemed brighter and Dorothy's step was a little lighter as she made her way to the parking lot. Dorothy took a breath in and felt the tension in the back of her neck dissolve. She now knew she had a great future in store once they got through the next several days. She had deliberately avoided telling Ethan about moving into the Manor knowing he would never approve. She knew he was right about the bike, though and resolved to do something about it immediately. On her bike, Dorothy went to the service station owned by her brother Matt. Billy was on duty again and his smile went from ear to ear when he saw Dorothy.

"Hello Billy, how are you doing so far today?" Dorothy asked after she took off her helmet and remained sitting on her bike.

"So far so good, Aunt Dorothy." Billy nodded. "No problems so far today."

"Good Billy. That's good. Is your father here right now?"

"No, Aunt Dorothy, he's still at the Manor. He said he would be along to help close up this evening. Why, what's up? Maybe I can help." The eagerness in his eyes made Dorothy smile.

"Okay. I would like to park my bike here after I take the trailer to the Manor to unload it." Dorothy said.

"No problem! We have a compound in the back that is locked and chained. It should fit nicely in there with a cover over it to protect it. But what are you going to drive if you park your bike?" Billy asked.

"Well Billy, it looks like I am going to have to buy a car. Do you have any idea where I could purchase a good one?" Dorothy asked. Billy's beautiful smile was back on his face again.

"Boy, do I! I have a friend who is trying to sell his muscle car and . . . ."

"No, Billy. No muscle cars." Dorothy interrupted.

"Oh, okay. What type of car do you like?"

"A small new or used SUV would be nice. Blue is a nice color."

"Are you going to trade in your bike?" Billy asked.

"No, it's not necessary. Besides, I could never sell my bike, Billy, you know that."

Billy thought for a moment and then came up with an answer. "Well, there is the Ford lot, the Chrysler lot, the Toyota lot, and the GM lot. Or you could just go to the used car lot." Dorothy rolled her eyes.

"That's a lot of choices, Billy. I guess I'll have to take someone with me when they have the time and go car shopping after I get my belongings unpacked." Billy thought for a second then smiled again.

"Can I go with you?" He asked. "I get the day off tomorrow and we can take my car."

"Sure. As long as you don't enjoy it too much. You know Grandpa's funeral is on Wednesday."

"I know. I will show respect Aunt Dorothy, but you need someone with you who knows cars. And I would like to help." Billy's brown hair began to blow in the breeze. Dorothy was touched that he wanted to help and highly amused that he thought she didn't know what to look for.

"*I guess he will find out tomorrow.*" She said to herself. To Billy she shook his hand and said "Be there early in the morning but not before nine. You know how Grandma likes to have her morning routine uninterrupted."

"Yes ma'am!" Billy hooted and ran to help the car that drove up to the pump. Dorothy took her bike around to the bay doors on the side of the shop. They were open and there was a mechanic working on a car on the hoist.

"Hello!" Dorothy called out.

"Yes ma'am!" A man Dorothy had never met before came out into the sunshine while wiping his hands on a greasy rag. "What can I do for you?" His dark brown hair was ruffled and dirty, his scruffy beard was several days old, but his coveralls covered his lean frame quite well and his smile earned a little trust with Dorothy.

"I need to hitch my trailer up to my bike. Do you think you can bring it out so I can do that?"

"Sure. Just give me a moment." He tucked the rag in his back pocket and went back inside. From the back of the shop Dorothy could hear some noises and soon, the man appeared pushing her trailer in front of him while holding onto the hitch. "Here you go. Now let's see, how does this hitch work?" He bent down to examine the hitch and Dorothy tapped him on the shoulder.

"I'll show you."

"Oh sure." The man stood up and backed away. Dorothy took mere seconds to capture the hitch on the ball joint and set the safety chains. "Wow! You have definitely done that before." The man stood back with his hands on his hips and a smile.

"Yes, I have. But thank you, Dean." Dorothy shook hands with the man whose name patch said Dean and waved goodbye.

"Nice guy." Dorothy thought to herself. "Not a typical redneck who thinks a woman should be barefoot and pregnant."

Dorothy kept her bike to the speed limit and took the lesser travelled roads to the Manor. She didn't want to attract attention to her fire engine red bike and trailer. She was taking Chief Barns' words of caution to heart. Dorothy was not going to let anything happen to her family.

Arriving at the Manor the dark little rain cloud that had crept up on the horizon had let loose and it began to rain. Softly at first, but by the time Dorothy had all her belongings in the foyer, she was dripping wet. So was her luggage.

"Well, look whose home!" Matt's smiling face came around the corner from the kitchen and he stood surveying the luggage in a sodden heap on the floor. "You know mother is not going to like the puddle on the floor." Matt reached for one of the bags with a smile. "Brent, come and give us a hand." Brent joined them from the direction of the living room where children could be heard laughing over the sound of a movie. Together the three of them struggled up the stairs with the luggage and placed it on the rug by the bed so the dampness would be absorbed by the rug.

"This is all you've got?" Brent asked. "There should be more."

"Why?" Dorothy asked.

"You're a woman! Women always pack everything except the kitchen sink." Dorothy punched his shoulder and laughed at the soft ribbing. Matt threw his hands up in surrender.

"I'm getting out of here." Matt left and went back downstairs. There was a pause as Brent and Dorothy heard their mother giving a stern reprimand to Matt for leaving such a mess on the floor. The two of them laughed as they heard the familiar sputter Matt made whenever he tried to get himself out of trouble.

"Seriously, sis. Don't you have anything else? No mementos, sentimental articles? Just clothes?" Dorothy moved over to the luggage and tapped the top of one.

"Some of this is not just clothes. I had a business in Toronto and I sold my half back to the company. When the luggage is dry and there's time, I will show you what I used to do for a living when I left the Forces." Dorothy smiled.

"Sure. I'd like that Dot." Brent gave Dorothy a quick hug and went back downstairs to leave Dorothy to unpack. She closed the door of her room to the laughter of the children and the wonderful smells coming from the kitchen. She needed a few moments to herself just to relax and unwind a little. The reaction from the news was causing her to shake a little from nerves. Taking off her shoes, she dried her damp hair in the ensuite in her room and laid down on the bed intending to rest for a little while. Her brain was on overload and when she finally drifted off, she dreamt of screaming cars, steel smashing into wood, and guns roaring as she returned fire on her attackers. One dream slid into another and she found herself back in Kandahar, her arms reaching for the one child she could never rescue. The sun, the sand, and the rifle fire were there in her dreams every night.

A soft knock on her bedroom door brought her awake and she sat up, the sounds of rifle fire echoing in her brain. Her mind cleared as another knock sounded on her door.

"Yes? Come in!" Dorothy called out as she wiped the cobwebs from her eyes. Her mother opened the door and stood there with a smile.

"You must have been tired." Her mother said with warmth. "You were out for nearly two hours." She raised a hand to Dorothy and beckoned her. "Come down and have dinner with us." Dorothy went to her mother and gave her a hug.

"I'll be right down. I just want to splash some water on my face and brush my hair then I'll be down." Dorothy said.

"Okay. But hurry. Maria made your favorite." Dorothy's eyes brightened at the words.

"Spaghetti and meat balls!" She exclaimed. "I won't be long, Mother." Temperance laughed at Dorothy's eagerness and left to go downstairs. It didn't take long at all for Dorothy to brush her hair, rinse her face, and hustle down the stairs to join everyone for dinner. She could eat spaghetti and meatballs anytime!

CHAPTER TEN

During dinner Dorothy told the family about her meeting with Chief Barns, while leaving out the part about being innocent. The children were once again absent as they had already eaten dinner and were happily in the living room playing video games and reading books or watching television. The door to the dining room had been closed but the adults could still hear muffled laughter coming from the direction of the living room.

Dorothy finished telling the family about the meeting and a silence descended over the table. It was broken by Temperance as she struggled to understand.

"You mean your father's death could be related to what happened fifteen years ago?" she asked.

"Yes. That's what Chief Barns said. He wants us to be on the lookout for Therese and anything strange or unusual." Dorothy nodded.

"Great! Not even here a week and already you are causing us problems again!" Patricia burst out.

"Patricia! She is your sister!" Temperance cautioned. "It is not her fault this has happened. It isn't anybody's fault. You cannot blame her for the misfortune that has entered our home." Her angry cautioning brought Patricia's angry outburst to a halt. Looking down, Patricia nodded.

"You're right, Mother." Patricia apologized. "Dorothy, I'm sorry." Dorothy nodded as Patricia swallowed. "It's just, well, it's going to take time to get used to everything and the change. I didn't mean you any harm."

"That's okay." Dorothy felt a lump forming in her throat as well. The urge to tell them all about the remainder of the conversation she had with Chief Barns sat heavy on her shoulders. "I understand."

"This is an opportunity for us all to work together as a family once more." Temperance stood and reached out her arms and took the hands of Dorothy on one side, and Matt on the other. "I want you all to stand up and take each other's hands." The remaining adult family members complied. "Now, I want you all to promise from this moment on we will act like a family the way our family should. We will respect each other and our differences will be worked out within the family."

"We promise!" Came the chorus. They all sat down and resumed their meal.

"Why do I feel like I'm back in boy scouts?" Brent asked.

"You were never in boy scouts. I was." Matt answered. "You were in girl scouts."

"Matthew!" Temperance scolded to the chorus of muffled laughter.

"Sorry Mother." Matt hung his head in mock shame.

"Dorothy, seeing as you are staying here once more, I would like you to help me organize your father's office and see if we can't find the resumes we have on file for a new housekeeper." Temperance asked.

"Sure Mother. I can do that. And until we find one, can we all help with the housework?" Dorothy glanced around the table. Everyone nodded.

"Is the funeral scheduled for sure on Wednesday?" Brent asked. Everyone looked to their mother.

"Yes it is. Chief Barns called and released your father's body and now we need to pick out his suit and I would like Matt and Brent to take it down to the funeral chapel in the morning." The rest of the meal talk consisted of who would be the pall bearers, who would do the eulogy and who would sit where in the chapel. The meal was finally finished and coffee was served.

"I could use help doing the dishes!" Evelyn declared as she stood up. All the men volunteered to watch the children in the living room while the ladies did the dishes. Maria was just not used to having so many hands in the kitchen all at one time. Temperance took her to the side to discuss the luncheon being held at the house after the internment at the cemetery. Soon, all the noise and clatter in the kitchen was finished and the ladies all went to join their families.

Temperance announced her intention to go up to the master bedroom and choose their father's burial suit. Dorothy went with her so she could speak with her in private. Once again behind closed doors, Dorothy went to sit on the bed and watch her mother go through the suits in the closet. With her back to Dorothy, Temperance glanced back over her shoulder at Dorothy.

"Okay, Dorothy. Out with it. What do you want to say?"

"How did you know?" Dorothy asked.

"You always get that thoughtful look on your face when something is troubling you. You've had that face on all during dinner and you are ready to burst so out with it."

"You always could tell when something bothered me." Dorothy smiled.

"Yes I could." Temperance left the closet and came to sit on the bed beside her daughter. She put her arm around Dorothy's shoulders. "Now tell your mother." Dorothy saw the love in her mother's blue eyes and didn't know how to start.

"Okay. There was more to the conversation with Chief Barns." Dorothy began. She told her mother everything.

"That's wonderful, sweetheart! I am so proud of you. But why can't we tell the others? They deserve to know that their sister is innocent."

"Chief Barns said if we go public with this information, the person we are looking for, Therese, will know we are looking for her so we may never find her. Chief Barns also wants us to keep a look out for anything unusual."

"Then perhaps it is a good idea for you to go through those resumes as soon as possible." Temperance said.

"You kept her resume?" Dorothy asked in surprise.

"Of course we did. Your father was very businesslike and organized. He did all the interviews, of course, but he picked the best one according to our needs. We never had any trouble with her all the time she stayed in this house."

"Did father do a background check?" Dorothy asked.

"I'm sure he did. I know he called all her references and she got stellar reviews."

"Okay, then I'm sure Chief Barns will want those as well." Temperance noticed something in the eyes of her eldest daughter when she spoke of Chief Barns. She slowly nodded to herself as understanding started to blossom in her mind. Her daughter was quite taken with the Chief of Police.

"*I wonder if Dorothy even knows it yet.*" Temperance thought to herself.

The two women stood and approached the closet together. They stood side by side discussing which of the suits her father would wear for his final public appearance. Dorothy noticed a tear in the corner of her mother's eyes and asked her if she wanted to be alone.

"Perhaps that would be a good idea. And don't hold tea for me, sweetheart. I think I will just retire early." Dorothy gave her mother a quick hug and went to the door. Before she could open it her mother called out to her.

"Dorothy!" Dorothy turned back to her mother with her hand still on the doorknob. "I want to thank you." Her mother's voice was barely a whisper.

"For what?" Dorothy's puzzled voice asked.

"For coming home and staying so strong. We need you here." Her mother's eyes were bright.

"You're welcome. Good night mother." Dorothy slipped quietly out the door and stood with her back against the wall to give herself time to clear the tears from her own eyes.

Dorothy knew it had been difficult for everyone when she went away. Some of the family felt she was guilty of the charges against her and she knew they needed the time away from her to change their minds. They could only see what they were told to see. Their father had been in control of everything in his life, even the minds of his children. If he wanted them to believe in something, they did. Most of the time that was a good thing but the one time Dorothy needed him to believe in her, he didn't. His beliefs rubbed off on his children and they believed it for over 15 years. It would take time to change those beliefs but the process had finally begun. Dorothy felt she could afford to be patient.

CHAPTER ELEVEN

The day of the funeral arrived and the sun was hidden behind gray clouds damp with grief. It felt so surreal for Dorothy to know that she was finally going to see her father after a fifteen year absence and it would be the last time she would see him. Dorothy would never be able to tell him of her innocence and that she didn't hate him. She wanted to be able to tell him what a success she had become in the security business. Dorothy also knew she would no longer be able to tell him. This thought brought tears to her eyes. The family had been placed in the ante room of the Memorial Hall while they waited for the guest to arrive and settle in. Finally, the room was silent and the family gathered to walk up the center aisle with their mother supported by Brent and Matt. As they slowly walked up the aisle and Dorothy passed people she used to know, she saw the whispers behind their hands and the pointed fingers. Dorothy held her head higher when suddenly Patricia and Evelyn moved up on either side of her and slipped their arms around her. The Adams family wanted everyone to know they loved and supported every member of their family. Dorothy was grateful for the support.

They stopped in front of the open casket before they sat in their seats. The three sisters with arms intertwined, gazed at the solid and stern countenance of their father's face. Even in death he couldn't smile. Dorothy saw the man she used to know. The strong and silent face so unforgiving, but yet so loving at times. He was a little grayer, but his presence was still just as fierce as the day Dorothy left Redwood. Patricia and Evelyn urged Dorothy to her seat and they sat as they had stood; arms around each other. Tears and tissues were evident in plenty as everyone settled and waited for the service to begin. Dorothy noticed her mother looking around before reaching for a fresh box of Kleenex and caught her eye. Temperance rested her eyes on her eldest daughter and smiled her support for Dorothy.

After the service, the family slowly followed the casket out to the hearse and then to the cemetery. Dorothy noticed Chief Barns was there on the outside of the crowd, dressed in civilian clothing. He wore sunglasses even in the cloudy weather. He wore a dress shirt and a sports jacket with jeans and black cowboy boots. His six two frame was broad shouldered and trim at the waist. Dorothy noticed the wind ruffling his sandy blond hair just before she closed her eyes for the prayer.

"This is crazy. This is really crazy! I shouldn't be thinking about Barns while I'm standing at my father's graveside." Dorothy thought to herself. The minister walked up to their mother and expressed his sympathy to her then turned to leave. Dorothy opened her eyes and waited her turn to throw her rose into the open grave. Once again the three sisters flanked each other as they filed back to the limos.

"Miss Adams, may I have a word with you, please?" Chief Barns had come up quietly behind them. Dorothy paused as if startled and then turned to face him. Patricia and Evelyn stayed by her side.

"Now? You want to talk now?" Dorothy whispered as they stepped to the side.

"I need to know if you have noticed anything unusual." Chief Barns whispered back.

"Look, I just buried my father. Now I have to escort my mother and the rest of my grieving family back to the Manor where we will never be greeted by our father ever again. Can't this wait until later?" The grief and the pain was evident in Dorothy's eyes. Chief Barns nodded and backed away.

"Yes ma'am. I'm sorry." Chief Barns seemed properly contrite as he turned to go back to his cruiser.

Dorothy stepped into the limo and shook her head. *"Fool couldn't even wait for a couple hours. Not very considerate of him."* She thought to herself. She lowered her head trying to deal with the dull headache that seemed to emanate from behind her eyes. Patricia and Evelyn glanced at each other then back at Dorothy. They began to smile in silence as Dorothy laid her head back on the headrest, not even noticing.

The next couple of hours went by in a blur. Dorothy thought the receiving line would never end. When it did, she walked into the kitchen looking for a fresh cup of coffee. Some of the ladies from the community had volunteered to host the luncheon for the family and had made sandwiches, casseroles, deserts, and drinks. One of them found a clean mug for Dorothy and poured her some coffee. Dorothy accepted it gratefully and sat at the table in the kitchen to stay away from the noise and conversation. Sitting down with the mug in front of her, Dorothy held her head in her hands and closed her eyes. The ladies in the kitchen continued to replenish the food and drink and came and went quietly through the swinging doors.

Dorothy took the first deep breath in days and felt the tension begin to slowly fade in her body. Her father's face swam before her eyes filled with anger and righteous indignation when informed of his daughter's part in the crash. The subsequent sentencing and juvenile detention, her enlisting in the armed forces, and her travels abroad, were all excuses as to why she hadn't tried to contact her father. She sent letters to her mother but sometimes they came back unopened. It had been her father's doing so his wife wouldn't be reminded of the absence of her daughter. It took fifteen years for Dorothy to understand that. But until then, the hurt, anger, and the betrayal she felt had kept her away from the family she had needed for so long. Tears started to stain the table top as Dorothy quietly started to cry. It all washed over her as Dorothy finally let it go.

CHAPTER TWELVE

The room grew quiet as Dorothy struggled to compose herself. She sat cradling her head in her arms while she felt the loss of a sternly disapproving father; a father who would never be able to see how successful she was or learn of her innocence so long ago. Admittedly she had been drinking but that mistake should not have cost her a lifetime with her family. Her mother had quietly come into the room after being alerted by one of the ladies doing the serving and she sat beside Dorothy. Slipping her arm around Dorothy's shoulders she held Dorothy until her sobs had subsided. Looking up into her mother's damp eyes with her own tear stained ones, Dorothy wiped the runny mascara away with the back of her hand, making an even greater mess.

"I should have come home after Kandahar." Dorothy said.

"No sweetheart, you weren't ready yet." Temperance smoothed the matted bangs from Dorothy's eyes and kissed her brow. "Everything happens for a reason. You didn't come home because you had to prove yourself." Temperance held tight to her daughter as if afraid she let go, Dorothy would be gone again.

"I had to prove myself to my father but he never found out how I did." Dorothy's answer was muffled as she buried herself deeper into the embrace that she had missed so badly.

"No, child, you had to prove your worth to yourself. Your father knew all about you. And he couldn't have been more proud." Dorothy sat back and held her mother at arm's length.

"What do you mean I had to prove my worth to myself? And are you also telling me my father knew about my career? What I did? How?" The questions that Dorothy voiced were confusing to her.

"Listen for a second before you react." Temperance smoothed the hair from Dorothy's brow again then cupped her face in her hands. "Your father followed your every move." Dorothy's face registered her surprise. "He knew of all your successes and your exploits. I know he didn't approve of what happened so long ago, but he was never more proud when you managed to change your life around."

"How did he know, Mom?" Dorothy took her mother's hands from her face and held them in her lap. "And why didn't he say something?"

"Your father used the services of one of those IPs." Dorothy chuckled at her mother's mistake.

"Why is that funny?" Temperance sat back.

"It's called a PI. Or private investigator." Dorothy's wet eyes appreciated her mother's little slip and she smiled.

"Okay, a PI. He knew every step you took and every person you met." Temperance said.

"That doesn't tell me why he didn't say anything. He let me go for years believing he didn't want me around and that he disapproved of everything I did." Dorothy said.

"It wasn't your father's disapproval you felt over this but your own. You made your choices and your father knew the only one who needed to forgive you was you. It took some time, but you are here now."

"But mother, I was innocent of the charges against me, you know that." Dorothy's voice shook. "How could my father continue to act as if I was guilty, and let the whole world think of me the same way?"

"But the whole world didn't think of you that way. You went out and found yourself in a world where you were accepted as very strong, and hard working and honest. It was only here, in Redwood that you felt that way. And now you are home." Comprehension dawned in Dorothy's eyes.

"The letters he kept returning?" Dorothy asked with her eyes closed as if afraid of the answer.

Temperance didn't seem to understand the question and she looked confused.

"What letters? The last five years we never received one letter from you." Dorothy opened her eyes.

"I sent you a letter every other week and they all came back unopened. That is one of the reasons I didn't come home. I thought that if my letters weren't wanted, neither was I." The two women looked at each other in confusion.

"I never received any letters from you, my dear." Dorothy knew her mother was telling the truth. She would not lie about something so minor. But the fact that her letters weren't welcome did hamper her feelings of welcome in this house.

"Okay, Mother. It doesn't matter." Dorothy felt the mystery could be solved at a later date. "We have a lot of catching up to do over the next few days. And I am so glad I could be home for this." They hugged each other and sat back in peace. The rest of the adults in the family filed into the kitchen one by one. Coffee cups were replenished and after Dorothy rinsed her face so she didn't look like a disheveled raccoon, they all settled down around the kitchen table. The last guest had left so Maria had put the leftovers in the walk in refrigerator and had also gone home.

Dorothy felt at home sitting around the table and talking with her siblings and their spouses. It was very comforting to her to know she was welcome at her own home.

"Does this mean you are staying for good?" Matt asked. "You know we can find room for you somewhere in one of our businesses. What do you like to do and what are you good at?"

"Shooting people that tick her off and playing with guns, or so I hear." Brent said with a laugh. There was a general laughter all around the table.

"That's right, so tip toe lightly around me little brother. Especially if I don't get enough sleep." Dorothy pointed out. They all laughed again at the humor.

"We should all go to bed soon. We have the reading of the will tomorrow morning at 11 in your father's office. The lawyer said all of us adults should be there as we are all mentioned in the will." Temperance pointed out.

"Okay, mother. I'll make myself scarce tomorrow. Maybe I can go and find a used car, now that I am going to stay." Everyone clapped in approval except their mother.

"What do you mean, Dorothy? You have to be at the reading of the will as well." Temperance said. All the laughter stopped as they looked at their mother.

"What are you talking about?" Dorothy asked. "Everyone knows Father cut me out of the will."

"Well what you don't know is that a couple years ago your father put you back into the will." Temperance said with some satisfaction. All her children and their spouses seemed dumbfounded at this news.

"Why didn't he tell us?" Evelyn spoke out.

"Because he didn't want it to influence your sister's decision to come home."

"Oh." Dorothy sat back.

"Well now, maybe you'll be able to afford a new vehicle." Brent slapped Dorothy on her shoulder.

Dorothy tried to say that she really didn't need any of the inheritance as she was happy with the total in her bank accounts, when her mother cut her off without knowing.

"I think we should worry about that tomorrow and get some sleep tonight." Temperance said. She directed the other ladies in the room to help clear the table and the men went to make sure all the children were safely tucked in for the night. Dorothy still sat at the table as if stunned.

"Are you coming to bed?" Temperance asked her daughter.

"Yes, mother, I am." A slow smile spread across her face as she rose from her favorite spot at the table. It made Dorothy happy that no one seemed opposed to her receiving a share in the inheritance. Even though there was never a good way to tell her family about not needing a share in the inheritance, it was nice that no one opposed it. "I'm coming to bed now." A weariness seemed to settle on Dorothy as she walked up the stairs arm in arm with her mother.

"Do you think I could make a few changes in my room?" Dorothy asked her mother as they went up the stairs.

"Like what, my child?" Temperance asked.

"Everything!" Both of them laughed at that and quietly turned out the light at the top of the stairs.

CHAPTER THIRTEEN

The sun was hot the next morning and Temperance and the girls had to quickly set up chairs for the reading of the will in the office. Maria was once again pouring coffee and setting up lunch trays. Billy, oldest of the grandchildren, was keeping the other kids busy with games, books and stories. Dorothy glanced around her father's office at one point and wondered who would call it their own after today. Her mother had told them all that she didn't need to help with the family business anymore and would officially retire as soon as possible now that all her children were home.

Dorothy still hadn't found the right moment to inform her family that she was rich in her own right and didn't need any inheritance. She planned on living in Redwood but decided to start taking care of herself and her needs. Dorothy had decided she would sit on a board or something for the business but didn't want any more contact than that. She was going to live the life she chose and not what someone else told her she had to do.

"Are you day dreaming, Dorothy?" Evelyn asked as she started to clear the desk. Dorothy surmised she knew where every file was and every nuance of the hotel business.

"No, just reminiscing. Remember when we got caught in here playing hide and seek?" Evelyn's fair hair was swept up in a bun on the back of her head with little tendrils escaping on either side of her face. Her hand automatically went to her lips to hide the remembered laughter.

"Do I! As the oldest, Dad told us it was your fault we broke the cardinal rule. You got the switch while we had to watch. What made you think of that?"

"I remember at the time that it was worth getting the switch because I had won." Dorothy laughed.

"You did not!" Evelyn cried.

"I won!" Patricia called out as she entered the room.

"Didn't!"

"Did too!"

"Did not!" The laughter brought a smile to the lips of Temperance who stood listening by the window.

"Okay girls!" Temperance broke in. They all looked to her. "Time to get ready. The lawyer should be here in another 15 minutes and I want you all to be on your best behavior." She admonished.

"Yes mother!" They all acknowledged with complete guileless innocence. Temperance left the room with a smile on her face.

"I'm always on my best behavior!" This was from Evelyn.

"Are not!" came from Dorothy.

"Are too!"

"Not!"

"Oh geese you two, grow up!" Patricia laughed as she left the room.

"Come on, Dorothy!" The rest of them left the room and went to their bedrooms to get ready. Dorothy didn't have much to choose from but black leather definitely wasn't a good thing to wear at a reading of a will. She did have a pair of black jeans and a dark sports jacket. She felt bad that she hadn't had time to go shopping but she would remedy that as soon as she could.

Downstairs the doorbell rang and Dorothy knew it was time. She slowly went down the stairs to join the others. She tried to take a seat in the back row but Temperance asked that all the girls be in the front row with her. Chairs scraped and murmurs were heard as each of them rearranged themselves in the preferred seating arrangement. Dorothy glanced at the grey haired gentleman sitting in the chair behind the desk. He was tall and thin and in a beautiful charcoal grey suit and tie that just shouted he came from money. There was an elegance about him and a quiet dignity that seemed to speak well of his character. Clearing his throat he picked up the papers in front of him.

"All right, let's get started. For those of you who don't remember me," he glanced at Dorothy, "I'm Jim Marshall, your father's long time attorney. I am sorry to meet you all again at this time. Your father's passing has left a hole in the business community and his shoes will be hard to fill." He started to ramble on about all the legalities and death taxes, estate fees, and his fees. Finally he came to the part where the rest of the estate was to be divided between his children and his wife. Dorothy tensed in anticipation of bad news.

"Now Matt, your father, asked me to make a change to his will a while ago so that his daughter Dorothy was once again included. So here we go." Jim Marshall started to appear nervous.

"To my wife, I leave a trust in the amount of $2 million dollars." A gasp went around the room at the unexpected amount. Even Temperance was astounded. "Another trust of $1 million has been set up for all the grandchildren so they can attend the college of their choice." He cleared his throat again. Temperance reached out and held Dorothy's hand on one side and Evelyn's on the other. "To my children I leave the following: each of you will receive an equal share of the family business and the finances required to run the said business." Dorothy started to breathe a little better in relief. Now the only thing that remained was the Manor. The family home where they had all grown up, lived, breathed, dreamt, and laughed. Dorothy assumed it would go to their mother, along with all the land it stood on.

"Now, the Manor Estate. It is bequeathed to my oldest daughter Dorothy." Another gasp went around the room.

"No, it should go to Mother!" Evelyn cried. She looked at Dorothy with an accusation in her eyes. "You don't deserve the Manor. You haven't been here for the last fifteen years." The look of anger in Evelyn's eyes unnerved Dorothy. Before she could answer to the accusation the lawyer stood up and raised his voice.

"Enough!" Mr. Marshal called out in a stern and commanding voice. "Let me finish!" The disapproving voices were silenced as he sat back down. "This is Michael Joseph Adam's will. It is what he wanted. Now shall we continue?" Dorothy looked down and felt sick. Temperance knew what was coming and squeezed Dorothy's hand in support.

"Okay. The Manor Estate and all its land, chattels, and mineral rights are bequeathed to Dorothy with the provision that Temperance Rose, my lovely and beautiful wife is allowed to live in it until it is her time to join me." Mr. Marshall cleared his throat again. "Dorothy will also not be able to sell the said estate, property, or mineral rights even after my wife's death. It is to be maintained and kept in the family for all of my children to enjoy and share." Dorothy heaved a sigh of relief. "I give this to my daughter Dorothy in the hopes she will be able to remain in the family and help maintain the legacy I leave to all my children." There was more legal issues to deal with and after that was dealt with, Jim Marshall stood and came around the desk to their mother. He stooped and took her hand in his own. He kissed her knuckles and gazed into her face with sympathy and genuine sorrow.

"I'm so sorry Michael has passed, Temperance. Please call on me any time you need my advice." And with that, the dignified, gray haired lawyer was gone. Evelyn rose from her chair and stood in front of Dorothy.

"I am so sorry for my outburst. It won't happen again." They both stood and Dorothy hugged her younger sister.

"It's okay. I understand. I didn't even know he put me back in the will." Dorothy looked around and knew it was time to tell them her little secret.

"All of you please, don't go! I need to tell you something. I should have told you sooner, but there never seemed to be a good time." The procession of family members to the kitchen for refreshments halted and they returned to their places. Their expectant faces all turned to Dorothy for her announcement.

"When I left the forces, I invested in some stocks, and started my own little security business. It was a successful business but it grew too big for me and I sold out a couple months before Matt here, called me to come home. So if some of you are upset I was included in the shares of the family business because you think I don't know how to run a business, you're wrong. With my proceeds from the sale of the business, I liquidated my shares in some of my stocks and came home. I don't need the money our father just gave me. I don't need the share of the business or the Manor, either. If you guys want, we can reinvest in the business and someone else can take care of the Manor."

"Well, now, isn't that interesting." Matt began to smile. "You actually know how to make investments in stocks?"

"And you ran your own business?" Brent asked with another smile.

"What kind of business?" Evelyn asked.

"What kind of stocks did you invest in?" Patricia added to the list of questions.

"Whoa!" Temperance stood beside Dorothy as she faced the horde of questions. "Give your sister time to answer each question. You're overwhelming her!"

"I've got an idea," Brenda, Matt's wife, spoke up. "Let's go to the kitchen and talk. I need a cup of coffee, how about you?" She put her arm around Dorothy's shoulder and ushered her through the family which parted to let them through and followed them into the kitchen.

Sitting her in the chair at the head of the table, Brenda brought Dorothy a plate with sandwiches and a pitcher of coffee and placed them in front of her.

"I don't think I should be sitting here at the head of the table. This is Mother's spot. She's the head of the family now." Dorothy tried to rise but Brenda shushed her with a wave of her hand.

"You sit there and start talking. You surprised us all in there and you get to sit there where we can all see you clearly while we listen." Dorothy looked around and started to smile at the faces of her family gathering around her.

"Come on, spill!" Brent called out. Temperance sat to Dorothy's right with a little smile on her face as well.

"Okay, well, I guess I will start with my business. It was a security business. We provided security for celebrities, business men, etc." Dorothy began.

"What kind of security?" Rosie, the quiet one spoke up.

"Personal security. Body guards, if you will. We also had surveillance systems and products that we would install and maintain."

"What celebrities did you help?" Robert, Evelyn's husband asked. Dorothy looked at him and smiled.

"I can't tell you. Client confidentiality."

"Oh. Okay." The disappointment was evident on his face.

"We did a lot of work for the city and that's very helpful when you are promoting your own product. But that side of the business got too busy and I knew it wasn't what I wanted. I went to my partners, they bought me out, and now I'm here." Dorothy held her hands out and shrugged.

"How much did you get for your share of the company?" Matt asked. Dorothy hesitated.

"$1.5 million." Came the answer.

"Look at you!" Brent kidded. "You are all grown up with a bank account and everything." He gave Dorothy a little punch in the shoulder.

"So you really don't need any of the finances of the company." Evelyn called out.

"No. I don't." Dorothy confirmed.

"And you came home anyway. Not because you needed your family's help but because you wanted to." Temperance pointed out.

"Yes, Mother. I felt it was time."

"Cool!" Mark, Patricia's husband said. "Now, what stocks do you own and will you teach me how to invest? I'm not very good at that sort of thing."

The rest of the meal was spent talking about the future and who would take care of what aspects of the business. The other children in the family all had their own businesses to run and found that adding the running of the family business might be a little too much for one person. They decided that they would form a committee and meet once a month to make business decisions or whenever it was needed.

"Dorothy, are you ready to take on the mantle of Executive?" Patricia asked with a smile.

"Actually, just because I don't have a family or a social life doesn't mean I don't have plans." Dorothy smiled back. "I can help but I don't want to take on the leadership role. Can we find someone we trust to do just that?" Dorothy queried the family.

"What were your plans?" Matt asked. Dorothy looked around the table while the other family members waited patiently for her answer.

"It doesn't really matter. We have to deal with the events in front of us...."

"I believe your brother asked you a legitimate question." Temperance interrupted. Dorothy tried to shrug off the question but no one would let her do it.

"Okay, I want to write and make money off the internet." Dorothy finally answered as she threw hear arms up in defeat.

"Can you really make money off the internet? I heard there are a lot of scams out there. Don't you have to be careful, sis?" The question surprised Dorothy. She was used to having people laugh at her goals, not ask about them.

"With the right product, you can make a lot of money, but you have to work at it." Dorothy answered.

"Well then, we will have to see if we can find someone else to lead the family in the business." Brent said.

"How about we talk to Jim Marshall and see if he can help us out?" Temperance understood Dorothy's unwillingness to step in to the role. She had her own plans.

"Do you think he would be willing to help until we find someone?" Matt asked his mother.

"Yes, of course. He is the Executor of the will, and he has been with your father for as long as I can remember."

"Okay, then, why don't we do that?" Dorothy asked. "And as soon as we can, we will set up a meeting with him to go over our views on how we want the business to go."

"And we will make sure we know every little thing about the business. Can we get some financial reports as well?" Brent, always the business man, asked his mother.

"All right. I will call Jim Marshall and request all these things. But we will do this tomorrow. The rest of the day should be spent with the children in the other room." Temperance pointed out to her children.

Dorothy helped Maria clean up the kitchen while the others went to see to their families. It didn't take long but it gave Dorothy a chance to reconnect with Maria.

"I am so glad you are home, Miss Dorothy. I've missed you."

"I missed you as well, Maria. How is your family?" Dorothy hugged her as they went about their tasks.

"Are you going to stay?" Maria asked. The hope was evident in Maria's round little face and Dorothy nodded yes.

"Of course. I couldn't stay away any longer. I missed your spaghetti and meat balls!" The two of them continued to kid around while immersed in their tasks until Maria made a comment that made Dorothy pause.

"I wish Therese were here to help. I am getting too old for this. She was not very helpful at first when she came but now it seems we cannot do without her." Maria gave a sorrowful shake of her head.

"Do you mean she didn't have much talent as a housekeeper?" Dorothy asked.

"Oh no! This was her first job and she was very excited to be here. It did not take long before she was very good." The sun coming in the large kitchen window seemed to give Maria's dark hair a halo as she stood before it. Her apron was damp and had a few stains on it and it covered a cotton housedress with a light yellow flower pattern. The sensible shoes completed Maria's ensemble and gave her the air of a traditional cook for a large family. Dorothy had always loved sitting in the kitchen working on her homework when Maria was cooking the family dinner and that seemed to bring the two of them closer together than the rest of the family.

"So, where did she come from?" Dorothy asked.

"I do not know. Only Mr. Adams knew. She never talked much about herself. She was always asking questions on how to do her job better and was a very fast learner. She had enthusiasm, is what Mr. Adams called it. The desire to be the best at what she did. That is why he hired her."

"I see. Okay. Well then, did you meet any of her friends?" Dorothy asked another question. She knew that Chief Barns would appreciate any little bit of information and Maria didn't seem to mind the questions.

"I do not think she had many friends." Maria thought. "But she did like to go to the library on her days off. She liked to read so much."

"What kind of books did she read?"

"I do not know. She brought her books home in a book bag." Maria turned to Dorothy with a knowing smile on her face. "I was not her mother. She was courteous, friendly, and hard working. She even showed me respect. If you must know what kinds of books she read, Dorothy, you can talk to the librarian. And do not think I didn't know you have been, what the word is, interrogating me." Maria stood with her hands on her hips while she admonished Dorothy.

"I'm sorry, Maria. It's just, I can't figure out why this well liked and trusted housekeeper who loved her job would just take off without telling anyone." Dorothy explained.

"You must talk to Chief Barns and tell him your suspicions." Maria went back to wiping the counter. "He is very handsome man, that Chief Barns." Maria's accent was always more evident when she was trying to joke with Dorothy. Maria's Mexican heritage and old world charm gave her an air of warmth and trust.

"Are you trying to match make for me, Maria?" Dorothy asked in surprise.

"He likes you, I can tell." Maria waved her pointer finger in the air. "And you like him."

"What makes you think that?" Dorothy asked.

"I have seen the way he looks at you when he thinks no one is looking. And I see the way you look at him. It is a good match." Maria confirmed her statement with a nod of her head.

Dorothy's mother came into the kitchen and heard the last part of the conversation.

"Maria, are you match making for Dorothy already? She just got home." Temperance laughed with the other two ladies.

"You may laugh, but I was right about the other four and I know I am right for her." Maria waved her finger in the air again as she continued her tirade. "I picked good boys for the girls and good girls for the boys!" Maria's indignation made her stand with pride in front of the two ladies.

"Okay, okay, Maria, you win." Dorothy laughed. "It's just that I don't think I'm ready for that kind of a relationship yet."

"Neither were your brothers and sisters but they listened to me anyhow." Maria turned back to her chores.

Temperance had come into the kitchen looking for Dorothy and wanted to talk with her in the office. They made their way there and closed the door behind themselves. Temperance sat at the wide mahogany desk with an unease that showed and Dorothy sat across from her.

"I don't know if I will ever get used to sitting here." Temperance's hands lovingly smoothed the top of the desk. "Your father cut a wide swath, my dear. And I do not think I am the one to take over. It would be too much for me, but not for you." Temperance looked up into her daughter's eyes. "You came home because we needed you. And you needed us just as much. Could you please take some time to help us out a little?"

Dorothy swallowed the nervousness she always felt when her mother looked at her in that no-nonsense-way and talked in that low voice.

"Mother, I mean Mom. Are you asking me just because the others have families and I don't?" Dorothy wanted to know.

"Of course. But I am also asking because the head of our family built business should remain in the family. Not with some handpicked mercenary executive who has no idea how to run our business."

"I really never wanted to do this." Dorothy stated with reluctance.

"I know. But you will have the knowledge and the assistance of your brothers and sisters." Temperance started to smile as she sensed Dorothy's determination wavering. "Sweetheart, this is your family asking you to do this. I cannot do it. At this point in my life I should only have to worry about attending teas, going for walks and taking a vacation every once in a while. I have raised my family, and now I would like to enjoy the rest of my life." Dorothy knew the wisdom of her mother's words. Throwing her hands up in surrender she stood up.

"Okay, okay!" Dorothy cried out. "But only until we can find someone to take over." Temperance smiled and came around the desk to hug her daughter.

"Right now, we must try to find help for Maria. I know the rest of your brothers and sisters will be going home tomorrow morning, but

Maria cannot do it all herself." Temperance sat beside Dorothy in the leather chair. "Do you have any suggestions?"

"Well, we could go through the resumes of the previous applicants." Dorothy shook her head. "No, they would be what, five years old?" They both pondered the problem until Dorothy looked up and smiled.

"Does the local paper still have that section in the classified, "Services Offered" Mom?" Temperance nodded. Dorothy stood again and went to the door.

"I'm going to go and get a local paper and go through the ads, and if I can't find anything I will place an ad myself. Until then, I will help Maria as much as I can, okay?" Temperance nodded happily as Dorothy went out the door and to the foyer. Brent noticed where she was going and followed her.

"Where are you off to, sis?" Brent asked.

"I am going to find a local paper and check the classifieds for a housekeeper. If I can't find one then I am going to place an ad for one myself." Dorothy answered. She pulled her coat out of the closet and put it on.

"Do you want a lift?" Brent held his keys up and dangled them in front of Dorothy. It's raining out again."

"Oh. Sure." Dorothy waved to him. "Let's go."

CHAPTER FOURTEEN

Chief Barns was not in a good mood when he went in to the office that morning. His car didn't want to start and he had to have a patrolman swing by to pick him up. The coffee maker was broken and wouldn't be fixed until next week, and the muffin delivery was late. As a man who liked routines, Chief Barns was not happy. To top it all off, the background check he had requested on the missing housekeeper at the Manor still hadn't arrived. Stewing in discomfort from his interrupted routine, he reached for the empty coffee cup without thinking.

"Damn! I want a new coffee machine!" He hollered in dissatisfaction. Just then a knock sounded on his office door.

"Come in!" He stated loudly.

The mayor walked in and calmly sat across from him at his desk. The Chief stood up to shake hands but was waved away.

"Mr. Mayor! What can I do for you?" Chief Barns tried to sound polite. He had a particular distaste for politicians as well.

"I want to know what you are doing about the situation at the Manor." The Mayor prompted with an imperious nod of the head.

"Now Mr. Mayor, you know I cannot comment on the situation. It's an ongoing investigation." Barns said quietly.

"And you know that without my approval, you would not have been hired for your job." The Mayor stated flatly and without humor. "So I want you to start at the beginning. What are you doing about that woman?" Barns did not like being blackmailed at all. In his mind, the reason why he got the job was because the town council hired him. Not the Mayor. Still, he was wondering why the Mayor was interested at all.

"Mayor, I will not comment on the investigation, but perhaps you can help me solve the problem by answering some questions." Barns leant back and started to drum his fingers on the top of the desk with his right hand. It created a loud noise on the metal desk top.

"What kind of questions?" The Mayor asked.

"Just who are you referring to as 'that woman'? The housekeeper?" A look passed in front of the Mayor's eyes. It was just a fleeting glance but the Chief didn't like it. Annoyance that the Chief did not know who he was referring to was what he saw. There was a silence and the Chief snapped out the next question out of his own annoyance. "Well? Who is it?"

"I was referring to that thing that drove into town on a motor bike of all things. Fire Engine Red. What kind of a woman would do something like that? My God she looked ridiculous!" Chief Barn's anger was evident as he struggled to keep his voice level.

"I will tell you what kind of woman would do that. Someone who doesn't have a care in the world. Someone who fought for our country and received two medals of commendation in the process. A woman who came home as soon as her family summoned her because they needed her. She deserves my respect and sympathy on the loss of her father." Properly chastised, the Mayor's grey eye brows raised as he glanced at the Chief after his little tirade.

"Obviously you are not able to keep your own personal bias out of this investigation. You do know she is a convicted felon?" The mayor still seemed to be looking down his nose at the Chief.

"She is not a convicted felon. She was charged as a juvenile and her file was sealed when she turned eighteen. Since then she has led an exemplary life." The Chief started drumming his fingers on the desk top again and it filled the silence engulfing the two men. Neither seemed to want to back down from their opinions.

"All right then, we are getting nowhere with this line of questioning. What about the missing housekeeper. How do you know she wasn't kidnapped by the other woman in question?"

"The other woman in question rides a motor bike, remember?" The Chief peered closely at the Mayor's reaction of distaste. "Besides, from what I can manage to find out from the interviews my men made, Dorothy Adams had never met the housekeeper." More silence as the Mayor digested this bit of information.

"I can find out all sorts of things from the back ground check on Dorothy Adams, but I can find nothing on the back ground check on the housekeeper. Except that you were one of her references on her resume." The silent inference made the Mayor sit up a little taller in indignation.

"What are you trying to say?" The Mayor's eyes seemed hooded and his gray hair almost stood up on end.

"So far, that means you are the only one who knew the housekeeper before she came to Redwood. Now what can you tell me about her." The clock ticking on the wall seemed to keep pace with the sound of Chief Barns' drumming fingers.

"I don't really know her much at all." The Mayor finally admitted. "She wrote to me and told me she knew my niece, who said I would vouch for her. She needed a reference and I gave her one after I met her and had a short talk." The Chief continued to drum his fingers. "I didn't see any harm in it." The clock kept ticking. "See here. What is happening over there anyhow?"

"As far as I know, Mayor, the Adams family just buried their husband and father and are grieving. Add to that the worry they have for their missing housekeeper and the fact that the preliminary autopsy shows that Michael Joseph Adams was poisoned, well then you now know as much as I do." Chief Barns stern disapproval showed through in his manner as he met the Mayor stare for stare.

The Mayor finally took a deep breath and nodded. "Fine then. Can I expect a report on my desk by Friday morning?"

"Can I expect a brand new coffee maker by noon today?" Barns decided to play politician in the hope it might garner him some new information about why a Mayor would vouch for someone he hardly knew so that person could gain access to a mansion and the family in it as a person of trust.

"Can the old one be fixed?" the Mayor asked in his imperious manner.

"No." came the terse reply.

"You will have a new one as soon as you send the receptionist out with a requisition form that I will sign before I leave. Will that suit you?" The mayor asked.

"That's fine. I will send you my report by Friday noon." The Chief confirmed.

The Mayor rose and took a step to the door then turned back to face the Chief.

"Chief Barns, I happen to think you are doing a fine job. I realize I should not have provided that young lady with a reference upon second thought. I pride myself in being able to read people and judge their character correctly. If I committed an error in doing so with that young housekeeper, then I deserve to be chastised. Not ridiculed."

"Anyone who prides themselves in 'judging' people incorrectly without getting to know them first does not deserve much of anything in my book." Came the Chief's reply. "And I have not ridiculed you. However, you have taken great care to point out exactly how you feel about a certain young lady you *also* do not know anything about. That, in my opinion, does not even deserve the wasted effort of acknowledgement. Good day, Mr. Mayor!" The Mayor went through the door as if his coat was on fire.

Elva the receptionist came hurrying through the door with a sheet of paper in her hand and a look of awe on her face.

"I don't know what you said to him, but we now have the purchase order signed and approved for a new coffee maker." Elva said. "You know how long I have been trying to do that?" Chief Barns kept his eyes on the papers in front of him and pretended to be busy so Elva couldn't see the laughter in his eyes.

"I said please." Chief Barns answered.

"Hallelujah and pass the donuts!" Elva said as she went charging out the front door.

CHAPTER FIFTEEN

Dorothy's first day as the head of the family's business was busy looking for a housekeeper to replace Therese. Brent had taken her to find the newspaper and she had even called some of the numbers for ads for cleaning services, asking for names of people they would refer to them. This was all to no avail. She was just about ready to give up when the phone rang on the desk beside her. She was temporarily working out of the office at the Manor to make things easier. When the phone rang, Dorothy reached over and picked it up out of habit without looking at the caller ID.

"Adams house."

"Miss Adams?" Tiffany, Billy's girlfriend and front desk clerk at the Inn sniffed into the phone and her crying was evident. "Is Billy there?" she asked.

"No, Tiffany. What's wrong? Is Todd bothering you again?" Dorothy was alarmed for the young lady.

"No. Well, yes, but that's not why I'm calling." Tiffany tried to stifle a sob.

"What is it, then?" Dorothy asked in concern.

"Well, Todd did show up this morning. He caused another scene before I could have him thrown out and one of the customers complained to the manager." Her plaintive little voice sounded so woebegone. "The manager had warned me about this the last time it happened and now he said he has to let me go." Tiffany hiccupped into the phone. "I just wanted Billy to come and pick me up. I don't feel up to walking home alone with Todd out there."

"You stay right there, my dear. I'm on my way. Why don't you go and have a cup of coffee in the café and I shouldn't be more than a few minutes. Then we'll talk. Okay?" Dorothy felt a surge of anger when she hung up the phone. She knew that Tiffany was a good employee and she needed the support of a good manager behind her. Not one who pulls the rug out from under her when she didn't expect it. Dorothy surmised it was easier to fire Tiffany than it was to get rid of the Todd problem. This was an aspect of the family business that Dorothy planned to change.

Borrowing the keys to her mother's car, she made her way to the Inn hotel in record time and went straight to the café. Tiffany was there being consoled by one of the waitresses who was on her break. Tiffany's head came up as Dorothy walked in and she saw streaks of mascara running down Tiffany's cheeks.

"Hi, Tiffany. I'm here now so let's get you calmed down." Dorothy motioned to the waitress for some coffee and she sat at the table, prepared to listen to Tiffany's side of the problem.

"Well, I was working a double shift and Todd came in. He knows he isn't supposed to come in when I'm here. Then he pushed in front of this really nice couple and called them names. He was drinking again and I couldn't stop him. The couple was really upset and I don't blame them. Bart came out from the bar and threw him out but not before the manager came out. The couple said that sort of thing should not be allowed to happen and my manager agreed with them. He gave them an upgrade for nothing and when they left, he fired me. Right in front of another couple that came in. Now I don't know what I am going to do. I was counting on my savings to get me through college next year but that doesn't look like it is going to happen now." The words came out in a torrent from the upset young lady and her tears started to flow all over again.

"Okay, sweetheart, let's see what we can do. First, you have to go to the ladies' room and cleaned up. Then I'll have a talk to the manager and see what we can do about getting your job back." Dorothy tried to console the girl as well as give her some hope.

"Oh no, Miss Adams!" Tiffany exclaimed in haste. "I don't want my job back. If I got it, then everyone would just say I was a suck up. And the manager is not worth fighting with for a job that he thinks I am unqualified for." Tiffany sniffed and showed a stiff back bone with her words.

"What do you mean he doesn't think you're qualified to work the front desk?" Dorothy asked in surprise. From everything she saw, Tiffany was definitely qualified to work the front desk.

"He thinks I'm just a glorified housekeeper." Tiffany said into her Kleenex.

Really?" A sudden thought occurred to Dorothy. "I am surprised he would even say that to you. But I just had a thought that might appeal to you then."

Tiffany looked up from her sodden Kleenex and hiccupped.

"What?" she asked.

"First, you have to go and clean up. Refresh yourself with some cool water and get rid of that mascara. Okay?" Dorothy encouraged Tiffany. Tiffany nodded and slowly left the table and Dorothy smiled after her. *'I definitely know of a better job for her.'* Dorothy thought to herself. *'I'm going to enjoy this conversation with the manager when I get back from taking Tiffany to the Manor.'* Dorothy hummed happily to herself as she drank her coffee.

Tiffany came back to the table a few minutes later and all the mascara streaks were gone but her eyes still remained red and swollen. Sitting down across from Dorothy she gave a big sigh.

"I'm sorry I did that." She said.

"Did what?" Dorothy asked.

"I didn't mean to blubber on your shoulder like that." Tiffany looked down into her coffee.

"You have nothing to be sorry for. In fact, I have some news for you that is going to make your whole day." Dorothy smiled at her over her coffee.

"What's that?" Tiffany sipped from her cup and looked at Dorothy.

"I am in need of a new housekeeper. Maria the cook can't continue to do both jobs and my mother is unable to handle it so I am going to ask you to work for me at the Manor." Tiffany's look of surprise turned to one of joy as she began to comprehend her stroke of good luck.

"You mean you don't mind if I work for you?" She asked in surprise.

"No, actually, I would welcome someone with your attitude and work ethic." Dorothy answered with a smile.

"Well, if it won't cause any problems, me working for the Aunt of my boyfriend, then I will take the job!" Tiffany smiled and held out her hand to shake with Dorothy.

"There won't be any problems, Tiffany. I have the utmost confidence in your professional standards." Dorothy answered. "Now tell me, how much are you making here?"

"Oh! Uhm, I'm making minimum wage." She said.

Dorothy sat back in surprise. "What?" To Dorothy's knowledge that was virtually unheard of in the industry.

"Uh huh! Any tips we receive we have to share 50% with the management."

"I see!" Obviously the manager was cutting corners where ever he could and abusing the employees as well. Dorothy nodded. She was definitely going to change that. The very first chance she got.

"Well let's finish our coffee and go back to the Manor." Dorothy instructed Tiffany. "There is much to do."

"Actually, do you mind if we have coffee at the Manor? This stuff taste like dishwater." Tiffany's eyes went wide as she realized she was talking to one of the owners. Her hand flew to her mouth. "Sorry!" Dorothy laughed.

"Okay. I like the coffee at home better myself." Dorothy paid and escorted Tiffany past the front desk where she waved at the manager as he was helping some new arrivals. The look of concern he gave the two women as they went by made both women smile.

They arrived back at the Manor and Dorothy led Tiffany to the kitchen where they were greeted with smiles from both Maria and Temperance.

"Oh good, you did bring her back here." Temperance went to Tiffany and hugged her as a grandmother would hug a grandchild. "We were concerned when Dorothy told us where she was going." Temperance took over and sat Tiffany down while Maria poured Tiffany a cup of coffee. Tiffany quickly raised the cup to her lips and inhaled the strong brew before she took a sip.

"Now that is coffee!" she exclaimed with a smile. All the women laughed. "Thank you so much Mrs. Adams. Maria, your coffee is the best in the city!"

"I've always said one can always solve any problem over a cup of Maria's coffee." Temperance took a cup and sat with Tiffany.

"Thank you Mrs. Adams. And you too, Tiffany." Maria responded.

"Mother, I would like to introduce you to our new housekeeper." Dorothy said with flair. Temperance's surprise was quickly replaced with joy.

"Perfect! I couldn't have asked for a better person myself!" Temperance smiled her approval.

"She already has some experience, and it won't take long to train her, Maria. As a matter of fact, she has already agreed to start today." Dorothy added.

"Oh no!" Temperance admonished Dorothy with a withering look. "She has had a bad shock and I wouldn't dream of making her work today. Starting tomorrow will be fine. Besides, we have to clean out Therese's bedroom for her." Both Dorothy and Tiffany looked surprised.

"We? You mean you want me to help clean the housekeeper's new bedroom?" Dorothy protested. "That's Tiffany's job!"

"I don't expect to be able to live here. I have my apartment downtown." Tiffany protested as well. All the ladies at the table drinking coffee looked at Tiffany in silence.

"Is there something wrong with the accommodations here?" Dorothy asked as she switched her attention back to Tiffany.

"No, but, I have all my belongings."

"What belongings?" Temperance queried. Maria just smiled. She knew the child had lost the battle before it even began. If Temperance Adams wanted Tiffany to move in, Tiffany was moving in.

"We have plenty of room to store your belongings if they won't all fit in to your suite downstairs." Temperance said and her tone was final.

"Oh." Tiffany began to smile again. "What will I pay for rent?"

"Nothing!" Dorothy quickly answered. "And your wage will be $15 dollars an hour. Sound good?"

"Really?" squealed Tiffany with happiness.

"Really!" Temperance Adams smiled at the happiness in the girl's eyes. "And now, let's finish our coffee and talk about when you can move in and when you can start." Temperance seemed to be able to handle the negotiations so Dorothy took the opportunity to go back to the Inn to talk to the manager. She pulled in to the spot reserved for employees and went inside. She walked straight to the front desk and stood waiting for someone to come to help her. A young teenager with his vest all wrinkled and his white shirt hanging out of his trousers came forward out of the office and smiled at Dorothy. His mussed up dark hair seemed to stick out at all angles.

"Hi. You're new here, aren't you?" Dorothy asked. She glanced at the spot where his name tag should have been.

"Yeah! I was hired half an hour ago." The young man said with pride.

"How much training have you had?" Dorothy inquired.

"Uncle Ron told me he would give me a crash course in the business so I can take over for him some day." The comments made Dorothy understand the real reason behind Tiffany's firing. Nepotism was a good thing if it was for the right reason. In this case it wasn't. Dorothy's anger flared again. The phone began to ring and the young man ignored it.

"Aren't you going to get that?" Dorothy prompted.

"Nah! Uncle Ron said all I had to do was make sure everyone who came in registered and that was it. I don't have to answer the phone." The young man's attitude stumped Dorothy.

"Where is your uncle?" Dorothy asked.

"He told me to tell anyone who asked for him that he was on his break." Came the answer. The phone kept ringing.

"Where does he go when he goes on his break?" Dorothy asked.

"The bar." He pointed down the hallway to the doors of the bar.

"Thank you." Dorothy had a full head of steam when she walked into the bar and the dimmed lights did nothing to hide the fact. Her anger preceded her when she spotted "Uncle Ron" at the bar. He was sitting side by side with Todd Belknap, of all people. Bart stood at the end of the bar glaring at the two of them with his arms crossed and his eyes mere slits.

"Hello Bart! How are you today?" Dorothy called out to Bart who was the bouncer. His head swung around and he spotted Dorothy and he began to smile.

"Hello Miss Adams. How are you?" He smiled and shook hands as Todd and Uncle Ron glared at the two of them. The bartender came over with a smile and introduced herself.

"What will you have?" she asked.

"Just a Pepsi for now." Dorothy settled at the bar and raised her glass. Todd and Ron were still sitting there quietly watching her. Bart and the bartender were doing the same thing. Lowering her glass, Dorothy sat quietly to compose her words before turning to the duo to her right.

"Ron is it?" she directed the question to the manager. "The phone is ringing at the front desk and your nephew doesn't know how to answer it." Dorothy stated in a flat voice. "I suggest you should go and answer it before I have to. Your break is over." Bart started to nod and so did the bartender. Ron just sat there without moving.

"I don't think you have any right to do that, b—h." Todd stood up and started to walk toward Dorothy. Bart took a threatening step forward. Todd stopped in his tracks.

"I have every right to do that, Todd. And you would do well to watch your language around me. You know how our last confrontation ended with no help from Bart." Dorothy said quietly. The memory of that last confrontation angered Todd even more. His face and even the tips of his ears turned red.

"Todd, I'll go to the desk." Ron reached out with his well-manicured hand and held Todd back. "Come on, let's go." Ron made to leave with his beer in one hand and his other hand guiding Todd towards the door.

"I would leave the drink if I were you." Bart suggested. "It's against the law for alcohol to be consumed anywhere except in here." Ron slammed the glass back down on the bar in anger.

"Todd, would you please stay here? I would like a word with you." Dorothy asked looking straight at Todd.

"What the h—l for?" Todd turned sullen. Ron hesitated.

"It's a private thing." Dorothy looked at Ron who turned with an oath and left.

"Please, sit. I won't hurt you." It was Todd's turn to hesitate. "Please, Todd." Dorothy patted the seat beside her. The bartender made herself busy and Bart stepped forward. Todd sat.

"What?" came his surly question.

"Why are you here Todd?" Dorothy asked quietly.

"Listen, b—h, I don't have to tell you nothing." Todd grinned from ear to ear.

"You had better watch your language around me or there will be another incident like the last one." Dorothy instructed Todd.

"You can't touch me. I can charge you with assault." Todd smiled in his confidence.

"Now who here would tell a lie like that?" Dorothy asked him and leant her head to one side as if waiting for an answer. For the first time, Todd realized the dangerous position he had put himself in.

"I'm leaving." He pushed himself away from the bar and turned to leave, running straight into the broad chest of Bart who stood still as stone with his arms crossed in front of him.

"Please sit down, Todd. We need to talk. Before you get yourself into more trouble." Dorothy said. Todd turned around and sat back down with a sullen sneer on his face.

"What do you want?"

"Who is paying you to upset the running of the hotel?" Dorothy asked. Todd's look of stunned surprise gave Dorothy the confirmation she needed. There was someone trying to cause problems for the running of the Inn and not just her. She surmised Todd was just playing a small part in the scheme.

"What do you mean?" Todd stammered. "I'm not working for anyone." A small sheen of sweat appeared on Todd's scruffy upper lip.

"You're a terrible liar, Todd." Dorothy drank from her glass. "I know a lot more than you think I do. I just needed your confirmation like the one you gave me just now." Todd remained silent for a moment weighing the words in his mind.

"I never hurt anyone." The words came out as if Todd couldn't hold them back. "I didn't murder the old man, if that's what you're thinking." Todd began to show more signs of nervousness. "Can I have a beer?" His tough guy demeanor was gone as he fought to maintain some kind of courage.

Dorothy nodded and waited for the bartender to place it on the bar in front of Todd and Bart moved to stand at the end of the bar.

"Now tell me everything. Right from the very beginning. You were trying to get Tiffany fired even before I got here, correct?" Dorothy promoted. Todd nodded and gulped some of his beer.

"I was contacted about causing some trouble so the current manager could gather some finances together and purchase the failing Inn." Todd confirmed. "I was told it would be a bonus if I could get rid of Tiffany in the process so Ron could bring in his own people one by one." Another gulp of his beer. "I did bust up your room and get Tiffany fired, but that's all I did."

"Who hired you?" Dorothy demanded.

"Ron. But he's not the head. He was always calling someone else to get instructions and my payment." Came the answer.

Dorothy sat a little straighter and pondered the situation. She now had proof of her suspicions but to come out in the open at this time would not take her to the person instigating the hostile takeover. She had three hotels in town to protect. The Inn was the first one the family ever owned and was their flagship. Destroying the reputation of that one would slowly destroy the entire chain. And her mother said it would be easy. Shaking her head she turned back to Todd.

"I want you to put all this into a letter, address it to me, sign it, and then I want you to do something for me." Todd nodded nervously as he looked over at Bart.

"Whatever you want. I'm sorry for what I did, but I didn't kill anyone!" Todd reiterated.

"Okay, Todd. I believe you. I also believe you are a very smart young man, smart enough to know when to quit and walk away, right?" Dorothy's piercing stare nailed Todd to his seat.

"Yes." He nodded and whispered.

"All right, I want you to write out that statement and sign it right now." A pad of paper and a pen appeared as if by magic from the hands of the bartender. Todd began busily scribbling his statement and Dorothy motioned for the bartender to refill his glass. When Todd was finished, he pushed the pad of paper over to Dorothy then drained his beer glass.

"I want you to help *me* now, Todd." Dorothy began. Todd's mouth fell open. "I need you to help me find out who it is that is trying to take over my family's business. And how Ron fits into this whole business."

"I can't do that!" Todd cried out. "It could get me killed."

"Really?" Dorothy smiled. "And how do you know that?"

"Your dad got himself killed, didn't he?" Todd stammered. "I don't want to end up like that."

Dorothy shook her head. "Todd, you are a small player. You don't know who the leader of this take over is, and why would they bother with you, anyhow?" Todd cleared his throat and drained his beer glass again.

"So you think I'm safe?" he asked. Dorothy gave a little laugh.

"Yes, I think you're safe." Dorothy waved the pad of paper with Todd's statement on it. "This is all we have. I won't press charges to instigate a full investigation if you play ball with me." Todd was starting to feel the effects of the beer. Dorothy motioned for the bartender to give him a shot of whiskey.

"So what do I have to do?" Todd started to slur his words.

"I want you to tell me every time you are asked to do something before you do it. Is that clear?" Todd nodded his acceptance. "And Todd, I will be watching you so close, all right?" Todd nodded rapidly. "If you tell anyone about our conversation, I will make sure you get buried so far in the prison system you will never come up for air." Todd's mouth dropped open. Dorothy left the bar and walked to the front office.

Ron's nephew was still ignoring the phone and having trouble figuring out how to register another nice couple. The door to the office was closed and Dorothy knew the time to talk to Ron was now. She walked behind the front desk and tried to open the office door. The nephew tired to get between Dorothy and the locked door. He physically pushed Dorothy back a step and his chin stuck out.

"You're not allowed in there." He said. Dorothy's eyes slowly squinted with a look that showed she meant business.

"Touch me again and you will be fired. Do you know who I am?" Dorothy queried him.

"It doesn't flipping matter. Take a hike!" Dorothy could hear Ron moving around inside the closed office and she began to smile. Bart suddenly appeared at the front desk. He moved around behind it and reached for a key from the pigeonholes and placed it on the desk in front of the young couple waiting. Ron's nephew had a look of amazement on his face.

"Please take this complimentary room on us, and register at your own convenience." Bart's well modulated voice and courteous manner impressed the couple as they reached for their luggage.

"Thanks!" They both cried in unison.

When they were gone, Bart turned and grabbed the nephew's wrist and forced his arm behind his back.

"I want you to go home and take the rest of your life off, do you hear me?" Bart growled at the kid.

Dorothy could still hear desk drawers being opened and slammed closed. "Hello Bart. Can you read my mind?" Dorothy queried with a smile.

"Nope. I just read the statement that little prick wrote out. I figured you were on your way to fire Ron. That's what I would have done." Bart's smile made his whole face light up. "Can I help?"

"Of course. Can you get this door open without breaking it down?" Bart reached for a paper clip from the front desk and proceeded to pick the lock. When the door opened slowly Dorothy and Bart were presented with a desperate looking man in the middle of a mountain of paper files and chaos.

"What do you think you are doing?" Ron demanded. "I'm calling the police!" He reached for the phone and Bart took one giant leap towards him while landing his hand on top of Ron's before he could pick up the handset.

"I wouldn't do that, Ron. This is your boss you are looking at." They both looked to the door and at Dorothy's disapproving gaze.

"Tsk tsk tsk! Ron, you made a complete mess. What were you thinking?" Dorothy stood in front of the desk and crossed her arms. Bart returned to the door and closed it.

"I was only doing my job!" Ron's legs seemed to give out on him and he sat in the chair behind the desk with a little oomph. He put his head in his hands and gave up. "I didn't think anyone would get hurt." He mumbled.

"Ron, I don't think my father's death was actually a part of the scheme you and your 'friend' seemed to have hatched." Ron looked up, his face as ashen as the white paper on the desk.

"I'm innocent of that." Ron said in fear.

"I know. But you know the police will have to investigate the connection anyway." Dorothy pointed out. Ron's head fell back into his hands again.

"I know. I guess I'm ready for that." Ron slowly stood. "How long do I have before the police show up?" Dorothy slowly sat in the chair across from the desk. Her petite frame suddenly didn't seem so menacing.

"Sit down, Ron." Dorothy directed. "I didn't call the police. Not yet." Dorothy continued to tell Ron what she wanted from him and what she needed him to do. It was much like Todd in the bar except Dorothy did fire Ron. She obtained a statement from Ron and promised him she would use it against him if he ever showed his face in Redwood again. The only reason she did that was the fact that Ron had a wife and a small baby at home who would have been devastated if Ron had been arrested. She also made it very plain that if she ever wanted to contact him again she would definitely be able to find him.

After Ron left, Bart looked around at the mess in dismay and then back at Dorothy as she sat behind the desk.

"Man, you're tough!" I think I'm going to enjoy working for you." Bart smiled. Dorothy smiled and sat back in the chair with her hands behind her head.

"Bart, have you ever worn a suit?" Dorothy asked with a smile.

"Whoa there, boss lady! I'm strictly jeans and t-shirt. If you need someone to fill in while you find someone else, I can help in a pinch. But that would leave the bar without security, and believe me, you don't want to do that." Bart's little protest amused Dorothy.

"Okay, then who would you suggest that we have on staff who could lead the rest of the employees?" Dorothy trusted Bart's opinion.

"Have you met Mabel?" Bart said after considering Dorothy's question. "In my opinion, she's the best. She lives on her own and today is her day off. She usually does the night shift but I think that is a waste of her talent." Dorothy nodded and reached for the phone.

"I have her home phone number on my cell phone if you'd like it." Bart showed her his phone.

"Thank you Bart." Dorothy used Bart's phone to make a call to Mabel at her home. Bart went out front to handle another guest who came to register. While Dorothy talked to Mabel and apprised her of the situation she also made it plain that if Mabel agreed to take on the manager position, she would have to start immediately and she would receive a definite raise in pay. Dorothy described the mess in the office so that Mabel would know what she was getting into.

"Thank you Miss Adams! I won't let you down! I can be there in less than ten minutes!" Mabel said excitedly. Dorothy hung up the phone with a smile on her face. Going out to the front desk where Bart was nervously trying to register a guest, she closed the door so no one would see the mess.

"Bart, could you use some help here?" Dorothy asked as she slapped Bart on the shoulder playfully.

"Yes I could, Miss Adams." Bart grinned with relief. I should be getting back to the bar anyhow." Dorothy laughed and shooed him away with a smile. Taking over for him she quickly logged in to the registry on the computer and entered all the necessary information and assigned them a room. Then giving the guests their key and pointing the way to the stairs or the elevator, they went away happily with their bags.

Mabel was true to her word and was there in just under ten minutes. Her gray hair had been styled carefully and she wore a light pink business suit with matching pink slacks. Her smile and confidence told Dorothy she had made the right choice. When Dorothy opened the door to the office so Mabel could see the mess, all Mabel did was clap her hands with glee and announce she wanted to rearrange everything her way anyhow. Dorothy told her she would stay to help her until Mabel had her feet under her and then Dorothy would have to leave. Mabel also discussed having a chance to bring all the staff remaining in the Inn to a staff meeting so they could go over some changes and Dorothy could meet them all. Dorothy agreed to that and then turned back to the front desk and the ringing telephone.

For the next two hours, as the afternoon shift arrived at the front desk to sign in, Dorothy was kept busy registering guests and assigning rooms. The head housekeeper showed up and was surprised at the changes but she also appeared very happy. Mabel had called her to come in. When she was informed of the raise in pay, effective immediately, she stood open-mouthed in surprise.

"Come on, Rita, we need to get this office straightened out too. There are schedules to redo and assignments to hand out." Mabel had obviously stepped into the role of manager quite effectively. When the young lady who took over for Dorothy showed up, Dorothy was almost sad to step away. She remembered the way she had worked for her father at the front desk up until she had gone away. It was a good memory because she knew she had been good at her job. However, fatigue began to gnaw at her after the constant activity and she went to the café for a quick coffee before she went home.

Sitting at the table in the corner reserved for staff members, Dorothy waved at the waitress. Almost immediately there were two of them standing there ready to take her order.

"Are we really getting a raise?" asked one.

"Are we getting a new manager?" asked the other. They both stood there in anticipation of Dorothy's acknowledgment.

"Yes. You are." Dorothy said to the first one. "And yes, you are." She said to the second one. "Now can I get a cup of hot black coffee and some toast?" The items were there almost immediately and Dorothy almost laughed out loud. She was almost finished her small meal when her cell phone rang.

"Dorothy speaking." She said into the phone.

"Are you going to be home for dinner?" It was her mother and Dorothy was thankful to hear her voice.

"Yes I will. Shall I come home now?" Dorothy smiled into the phone.

"Of course, dear. Dinner will be at six." Temperance smiled back into her phone.

"What are we having?" Dorothy queried.

"Food. That's all that matters right now." Temperance hung up the phone with a smile.

CHAPTER SIXTEEN

Dorothy arrived home a short while later. She had a short talk with the excited waitresses in the café before she came home. All the talking and information seemed to have given Dorothy a headache. Parking the car in the garage, she entered the house from the back door that led straight into the kitchen. Maria was busy at the stove and Dorothy paused to take a deep breath of pleasure.

"Pot roast! Yummy! Maria, you know how I love your pot roast!" Dorothy exclaimed as she hugged Maria.

"You love all my cooking!" Maria admonished Dorothy with a loving pat on the shoulder. "Now go so I don't get distracted and burn the meal." Dorothy kissed Maria's cheek and left the kitchen to go into the office. Her mother was there on the phone and she had a look of displeasure on her face.

"Listen, Jim. I am not the one to make a decision on my own about the family business. I have to bring it up with the family and we make the decision together." Temperance paused as she listened to the voice on the other end of the phone.

"I will talk to Dorothy and the rest and I will let you know as soon as I can." Temperance put the phone down with a firm hand as she glanced up at Dorothy.

"Sounds as if Jim Marshall just made you an offer on the Inn." Dorothy surmised out loud.

"And how would you know that?" Temperance asked her daughter. "Do you have ESP or something?" Dorothy sat in the chair across from her mother.

"Just some intuition and a working knowledge of how human nature works." Dorothy shook her head to ease the headache.

"I made a few changes at the Inn in the management sector and I figured we would receive an offer fairly soon, but I didn't think it would be this soon." Dorothy explained.

"Changes?" Temperance asked. Dorothy spent the next fifteen minutes telling her mother of all the excitement she had caused at the Inn amongst the employees still remaining. She also told her mother of her theory about someone wanting to take over the family business by destroying their first hotel's reputation. Dorothy's actions and tactics had put a stop to that unknown person's plans and she explained that person was now showing their true colors by coming out into the open with an offer.

"Well! You *have* had an interesting day, haven't you? I suppose we will have to get the family together and let them know." Temperance said.

"Yes, we will. But first, I need something for this headache. Then we have dinner. Then, dear mother, I will be the one to do the calling. I need to apologize for making these decisions spur of the moment but I had no choice. The family deserves to know exactly what is going on and make these decisions together. Right?" Dorothy looked at her mother with a smile.

"Of course, dear. There is aspirin or Tylenol in the medical cabinet in the main bath upstairs." Both women left the office and made their way up the stairs. Dorothy found the headache remedy she needed and slipped into her bedroom to freshen up for dinner.

She contemplated the fact that whoever the mystery person was who wanted to take over the company was moving very fast. She knew she was going to have to move just as fast. Back down the stairs she went and straight into the office. She made a phone call to a friend of hers in Toronto.

It was her old business partner Troy and she asked him for a favor. She told him about needing a background check on the family lawyer. She had a feeling there was something about him making the phone call with the offer for the Inn that she wasn't going to like.

"Okay, Dorothy, I will see what I can do. I can't promise you anything because what you are asking for could possibly be called crossing the line." Troy said into the phone.

"I understand that, Troy. But this is my family business we are talking about here. I've landed into a nest of vipers and I need to make sure I know who I can depend on." Dorothy said.

"All right. It may take a couple of days but I will get back to you as soon as I can." With that, Troy hung up and left Dorothy contemplating her position when her mother walked in.

"Maria says dinner is ready. Shall we go?" Temperance smiled at her daughter.

"Of course." Dorothy turned the light out and closed the office door. All this excitement and she hadn't been able to call Chief Barns to see if he had found anything out about their missing housekeeper.

CHAPTER SEVENTEEN

Dorothy and her mother were just finishing their morning coffee and breakfast when the phone rang summoning Dorothy to the table in the hall. Picking up the receiver she wiped the toast crumbs from around her lips and cleared her throat.

"Dorothy here."

"Good morning, Miss Adams." Came the deep baritone of Chief Barns. "How are you this morning?" Dorothy's toes began to curl in her shoes and her stomach started to clench at the sound of his voice. Taking a deep breath of annoyance at herself, she answered him in the best professional voice she could muster.

"I'm fine, Chief Barns. What can I do for you this morning?" Dorothy asked.

"I hear you had a little bit of excitement yesterday." He said.

"I did. And I handled it quite efficiently. There was no need for anyone to bring it to your attention." Dorothy's answer was very clipped and precise. '*I wonder who tipped him off?*' she thought to herself.

"I know you did and I commend you on that account. However, there is something I need to see you about and I would like a word with you. Should I come to your house or would you like to meet me at my office?" The Chief's tone brooked no argument.

"I would prefer if you came here; for privacy's sake." Dorothy answered.

"That would be fine. Say, in half an hour?"

"Of course, Chief. I will have Maria put on a fresh pot of coffee." Dorothy's nervousness did not stop her from being a good hostess. '*This way he will be on my home turf and I will have the upper hand.*' She thought.

"I will be there. Have a good day." The Chief hung up and Dorothy hesitated. His tone and attitude seemed friendly, but sometimes that didn't mean good news. Returning to the kitchen Dorothy asked Maria to put on some fresh coffee for the Chief's arrival.

Tiffany arrived shortly after that with her bags in tow. Dorothy opened the door to find a beaming Tiffany bouncing from foot to foot in excitement. She gave Dorothy an impromptu hug, paid the taxi driver for his assistance, and then proceeded to pull her luggage into the foyer.

"I am just so excited to get to work. I will do a good job for you, I promise . . . ." Tiffany kept up a continuous chatter as Dorothy helped her with her luggage and took her to her room. It was basically a two room suite which had been used as a housekeeper's office and bedroom. The office part had been converted to a sitting area when the storage room off the pantry was installed. A computer had been installed down there for convenience sake and that gave the housekeeper more room to live.

Tiffany's excitement increased as she removed her jacket and hung it in her closet.

"Is there anything you need me to do right away? I can unpack later." Tiffany offered.

"That's fine, Tiffany. You unpack and get everything arranged. When you're finished, you can ask Maria about the routines and she will show you where your supplies are located." Dorothy answered. Dorothy was about to go out the door with another impromptu hug from Tiffany when the door chimes rang.

"I'll get it!" Tiffany called out.

"No, Tiffany!" Dorothy said with a laugh as she held out her hands to prevent Tiffany from racing out the door. "You concentrate on yourself right now. I'll get the door." Dorothy knew the guest was probably the Chief. She made it to the door a few seconds later as a second sound of the chimes rang out.

"Good morning Chief Barns." Dorothy greeted him with a smile. *'Show him confidence and stay strong.'* She thought to herself.

"Good morning Miss Adams. Thank you for agreeing to see me this morning." He said as he was ushered into the foyer. Dorothy took his jacket and hung it in the closet and preceded him into the office and closed the door. The Chief took a seat in front of the desk with an amused expression on his face. *'She's posturing to show me how calm and cool she is. She doesn't want to appear rattled.'* He thought to himself.

"Would you like some coffee?" Dorothy offered.

"I don't mind if I do." The Chief sat forward. "But first, I want to assure you I am not here to interrogate you or cause you any problems." He said.

"Okay. Then why are you here?" Dorothy asked.

"I was hoping you would tell me what happened yesterday and if you think it had anything to do with your father's death." Dorothy's hand paused half way to the intercom to summon Maria with coffee.

"I see. Well then sit back and take off your hat, Chief. I have a story to tell you." Dorothy went through everything that happened and told it without emotion. From the confrontation with Todd, then Ron, and his firing, and then the promotion of employees from within the company. She left nothing out including her supposition that someone was trying to maneuver themselves into a takeover bid. When she finished, she sat back and waited for Chief Barns to say something.

"I thought as much." He nodded. I've been keeping an eye on that place over the last little while because of some rumors I've been hearing." Chief Barns confirmed. "I do believe you handled it perfectly, except for young Todd." Dorothy instantly stuck her chin out.

"What makes you think I was wrong about Todd?" Dorothy's closed look was difficult for the Chief to understand.

"I think Todd should have been brought in and questioned."

"If I had done that, it would have alerted whoever is behind this move that I was on to them. As long as they don't know, then I have the upper hand." Dorothy said.

"Okay, I will admit that sounds right. But I want you to let me know the moment he steps out of line again." Chief Barns agreed.

"Now, do you think this takeover bid has anything to do with your father's death?" Dorothy contemplated her answer for a moment then spoke.

"No, I don't. If poison was used on my father, then I have to figure the murderer was a female, as the statistics show females prefer poison more than men. It's clean, easy, and not messy. Men prefer to create accidents or use a gun or knife." Dorothy was matter of fact in her answer and it surprised Chief Barns at how much she sounded so detached.

"I think the person who killed my father had to have been in this very house, and had access to his medication. In my opinion, that could only have been the housekeeper. She is the only unknown factor, in my mind. Did you find out anything about her back ground?"

"No. The only information we have on Therese goes back to the day she applied for a position here as housekeeper. The mayor was on her reference list, and after I asked him discreetly about his involvement with the young lady, I was no further ahead. Apparently she was a friend of his niece's. We have been unable to contact the niece about Therese as she is out of the country on a holiday." Dorothy nodded and thought for a second.

"So you have no idea who she is?"

"No. None." Dorothy nodded to herself once more. *'I'm going to have to give Trevor a call again and seek his assistance one more time.'* She thought to herself.

"Well if that's all, then shall we go find that coffee?" Dorothy smiled to sweeten the invitation.

"Not yet." Chief Barns said. "I was wondering how you are handling everything." Dorothy's face held a puzzled look.

"What do you mean?" Dorothy asked.

"I have some information about the reason you were not allowed back to Kandahar." The Chief explained and nervously cleared his throat to continue. "It says you were treated for PTSD"

"So? What of it?" Dorothy countered.

"After everything that is coming down on your shoulders in the last couple of weeks, you seem to be somewhat withdrawn in your answers. Very matter of fact. So little emotion." The Chief prompted.

"Chief Barns, everyone handles grief and stress differently. I have handled it in my own way. My emotions, and my personal life are strictly off limits. If you have any questions about my sanity or my behavior, don't dwell on it. I am fine. I'm home where I should be when my family needs me. Does that make you feel better? I am not going to crack under pressure." Dorothy's tirade made the Chief sit back with a smile. "Why are you smiling?"

"I just saw the first spark of an emotion from you. It really is quite fetching when that spark comes to your eyes and you toss your head back." The Chief laughed. His answer confused Dorothy.

"Oh. Okay. Did . . . you want that coffee now?"

"Yes please. And you can rest assured that you can call on me any time when you need help. But from what I can see, you can pretty well handle your problems on your own." Dorothy's stomach began to cramp and her toes began to curl again; which made it extremely difficult for her to lead the Chief into the kitchen for the coffee.

Maria greeted them as they came into the kitchen and noticed the gleam in the Chief's eyes and the confusion in Dorothy's. Serving their coffee at the table, she left the kitchen to give them the privacy they would need to find out they were made for each other.

"*I wonder if they even know it yet.*" Maria thought to herself.

CHAPTER EIGHTEEN

Todd had gotten up late, as usual and left his bachelor pad in his parent's house with a huge hangover. He couldn't really believe he had signed that statement in front of Dorothy and Bart. His ill-humor with himself stemmed from the fact that everything Dorothy had said was true. He was disgusted with himself as he ambled down the alley behind the liquor store. He stopped and had to lean up against the side of the brick building wall and light himself a cigarette. Drawing in a deep breath he let it out and felt himself begin to relax. The next thing he needed was a cup of coffee. He dug into his pants pocket for some change when he heard the back door to the liquor store start to open carefully. Todd ducked behind the dumpster and watched.

A blonde haired woman looked out and glanced around as if she was afraid of being seen. Todd found this unusual and very secretive. No one was ever allowed to come and go from the back door of the liquor store due to security reasons. The door was alarmed as well. Only, when the woman quietly slipped out and went up the alley to a dark looking small sedan parked at the end of the alley, Todd realized the alarm wasn't going off. That meant she knew whoever was in there. Focusing on the woman and her movements, Todd realized she looked familiar, even from the back. She was of average height, maybe 110 pounds, and she moved like a dancer. That was when Todd recognized her. It was the housekeeper that everyone said was missing. Todd tried to commit the license plate of the car and the make and model to memory. The car was gone and Todd raced to the end of the alley on foot. It went in the direction of the mall and Todd pulled out his cell phone. He entered all the information into his cell so he wouldn't forget it and then found himself walking in the direction of the Inn. Maybe he could parlay this information into a free breakfast.

Todd walked in the front door of the Inn and went straight to the front desk. Mabel was there handling some minor employee problems and she recognized Todd.

"What are you doing here?" Mabel called out to him. "I thought you were told not to come in here anymore." Mabel asked.

"Not quite. Miss Adams said I could call on her any time of the night or day if I had some information she might need." Todd tried to sound like he was trying to help. Mabel paused in her suspicions and then nodded and picked up the phone.

She rang the Manor and the call was answered by Dorothy herself.

"Hello. Dorothy here."

"Miss Adams, its Mabel here. I have Todd Belknap here saying you told him to call you any time he might have information for you." Mabel listened for a moment and handed the phone to Todd in surprise.

"Hello Miss Adams?" Todd was polite and not surly at all. "I am sorry to bother you at home but you did say to call you if I had anything helpful to tell you."

"Yes, Todd. What is it?" Dorothy said into the phone and Chief Barns' interest was immediately heightened.

"I saw someone I think you're looking for. I don't want to say who over the phone. Can you come down to the Inn and meet me in the restaurant?" Dorothy was surprised at the way Todd was openly trying to be helpful. Still she was going to reserve her trust until she was sure she could trust him.

"All right, Todd. Order yourself something to eat on me and we will be there shortly." Dorothy hung up and Todd handed the phone back to Mabel.

"Thank you ma'am." Todd said almost absently. He hurried away and stumbled over to the restaurant to order himself the biggest breakfast he could find. Mabel stood there like a statue with the phone in her hand and her mouth open.

Rita came out of the office and noticed Mabel's stance.

"What are you trying to do, catch flies?" Rita smiled.

"That was Todd Belknap." Mabel pointed to the doors of the café closing behind Todd. "He actually said thank you." Rita stood with her hands on her hips.

"What the hell is he up to now?" Rita asked.

"I don't know, but whatever it is, Miss Adams approves. He was polite to her on the phone as well." Mabel finally hung up the phone and pondered the most surprising thing she had seen in a very long while.

"So what is wrong with that?" Rita asked.

"He was polite! Almost apologetic! That isn't the Todd I know. Whatever Dorothy Adams said to him yesterday, he sure is different today. I still think he bears some watching."

"Me too. Now let's get down to work on this new schedule." Rita went back into the office and Mabel followed.

CHAPTER NINETEEN

Dorothy and Chief Barns walked into the café and sat at the table with Todd, who was happily tucked into a huge breakfast.

"Oh, hi." Todd said around a mouthful of home fries. "This is good. Thanks."

Chief Barns tapped Todd on the shoulder and Dorothy ordered coffee all around. Todd looked up from his plate with a question in his eyes.

"Don't you think you should tell us what it is you wanted us here to say?"

"Yeah, in a sec." Todd swallowed and motioned towards the waitress that was pouring the coffee. When she had withdrawn, Todd wiped his mouth with his napkin and leaned toward Dorothy in a conspiratorial stance.

"I seen her." Todd nodded and smiled.

"Who?" Dorothy asked with her brows furled.

"That woman you're looking for." Todd answered. "Coming out of the back door of the Liquor Stop up the street there." Todd took a drink from his coffee cup.

"What woman are we looking for?" Chief Barns was beginning to get frustrated with Todd. "Speak up before I remove that plate in front of you."

"The lady housekeeper you keep saying is missing. If she's missing how come I seen her coming out of the back door of the Liquor Stop?" Todd sat back as understanding dawned in both Chief Barns and Dorothy.

"You saw Therese coming out of the back door of the Liquor Stop, when?" Chief Barns quizzed Todd.

"Right before I called Miss Adams here." Todd pointed to Dorothy. "I figured the information might be worth a breakfast." He took another bite of his toast. "And besides, Miss Adams was good to me yesterday, so I figured she could use the help." Dorothy looked at Chief Barns with a whimsical look on her face as she leaned her head in her hand.

"You're sure it was her?" Chief Barns asked.

"Yeah. She used to come around there usually on Sundays." Todd mumbled around the food in his mouth. "She was pretty and I like to watch the pretty ones. So yes, I'm sure."

"Which way did she go and did she walk, drive, or run?" Chief Barns' urgent tone of voice made Todd reach into his pocket for his cell phone. He pulled up the information he put into his phone and handed it over to Chief Barns. Chief Barns immediately called the office on his cell phone and put out a Be On the Lookout (BOLO) on the car, the housekeeper and the license plate. Handing the phone back to Todd, he rose to leave.

"That was good, Todd. It will help us find her." Chief Barns nodded and left. Dorothy, who had remained silent until the Chief left, now leaned forward to Todd as he cleaned his plate with his toast.

"It was good, Todd. Very helpful. Your breakfast was well deserved." Todd leaned back with his arm around the back of the chair in a cavalier attitude.

"Yeah, it was wasn't it?" Todd appeared very pleased with himself.

"Kind of makes you feel good, to help someone, doesn't it?" Todd looked at her with suspicion as he placed a toothpick in his mouth to chew on.

"Yeah, what of it?" His tough guy attitude was back.

"If you were to lose that attitude, clean up a little, and get a haircut I could probably use you around here a little bit." Dorothy was watching Todd's face go from belligerent to astonished.

"You want my help?" He asked in surprise.

"You need a job, right?" Todd paused before he answered.

"Depends on what I gotta do. No more of that spy crap I was into before." Todd answered. "I'm done with that."

"Even if it means working at a legitimate job?" Dorothy asked.

"Miss Adams," Todd sat forward and looked down at his empty plate. "Everyone looks at me and sees a trouble maker; a useless bump on a log. They have ever since my dad took off and left my mom and me. I couldn't get a legitimate job. My reputation always preceded me. I'm not as bad as everyone thinks." Todd took the toothpick out of his mouth and deposited it on his plate as if he was closing the door on his past.

"I would definitely take on a legitimate job if the pay is good and the employer is fair." Todd looked straight at Dorothy. "It's just, I ain't never had the opportunity before."

Dorothy nodded and finished the coffee in her cup. She thought to herself for a while and then sat forward.

"I can offer you a job but it is hard work and some days you won't like it." Dorothy started to smile.

"You would trust me enough to do that after what I did to try and hurt your company?" Todd asked in awe.

"Can I trust you?" Dorothy leaned her head to the side trying to decide whether she should or not.

"Of course. What's the job?" Todd asked.

"I need help around the house with the gardening, cutting grass, maintenance, etc. Are you game?"

"I'm good with my hands, and I'm not afraid to work hard." Todd nodded and began to smile.

"Do I have to wear a uniform?" He grinned.

"No, but a pair of coveralls would help keep your clothes clean if you want." Dorothy laughed and reached across the table to shake on it. "Could you do me a favor and apologize to Tiffany first?" Todd lost his smile for an instant.

"Aah, I don't know what to say or where she is." Todd hesitated. "Is that a deal breaker?"

"Yes! And I know exactly where she is. I can take you there." Todd thought for a second and nodded.

"Okay. I know I have a lot of apologizing to do so I may as well start now." He stood up from the table and brushed the crumbs from his lap. Pushing his chair in, Todd stood ready to leave and waited for Dorothy to precede him.

The two waitresses working in the café paused in surprise at what they were doing. Todd's reputation was such that a courteous consideration like the one he had just performed for Dorothy was so totally surprising they couldn't believe their eyes. Things just weren't the same with Dorothy Adams around. They looked at each other and smiled. They really liked the change.

CHAPTER TWENTY

Dorothy was itching to get back to the Manor and call the Chief anyhow, so she figured taking Todd there to apologize to Tiffany would be a good thing. She had to stop him from smoking in the car and really had second thoughts when the cross winds of the open windows wafted across her nose hairs. The old cologne and body sweat was choking her.

"When we're finished at the Manor for the rest of the day I would like you to take the time to get acclimated, find where things are around the house, and then go home and get cleaned up. My mother would kill me if I let you take on the job without first scrubbing you clean."

Todd looked down at his black sleeveless t-shirt and sniffed. Then he sniffed his arm pits and rolled his eyes. "Oh gawd! I'm sorry Miss Adams." He looked over at her and grimaced. "I didn't think it was that bad. I will clean up, I promise." He said with a sick little grin on his face.

"It would help if you didn't wear that awful cologne!" Dorothy joked with him as she drove up the driveway to park in the garage. They both laughed and Dorothy led Todd into the back door of the Manor.

Maria was busy at the kitchen stove and turned around when she heard Dorothy and Todd enter.

"Aaaaahh!" She screamed. Grabbing the frying pan that was beside her she raised it and rushed forward with a menacing stance. "Miss Dorothy, run!" Todd tried to back pedal to get out of Maria's way when Dorothy stepped in front of Maria, trying very hard not to laugh too much.

"Maria! It's okay!" Dorothy grabbed the frying pan from the shorter woman who instantly put a hand to her chest as if in pain. Steps sounded from the hallway and Tiffany and Temperance both came rushing into the room to aid Maria.

Dorothy sat Maria down at the table as Todd tried desperately to make himself as small as he could in the corner by the door.

Holding up a hand to her Mother and Tiffany who both stood there in shock, Dorothy surmised to herself she should have called ahead first.

"Mother, it's okay. I brought Todd here on purpose." She turned to Todd and told him to get a glass of water for Maria. Todd rushed over to the sink as fast as he could with an anxious look on his face. Coming back to the table he handed the full glass to Maria who took it carefully while she looked over her shoulder at Todd.

"Is it safe?" she whispered the question to Dorothy. Dorothy laughed and told her to go ahead.

"Mother, Tiffany please have a seat. Todd has something he would like to say to Tiffany." Todd stood there open-mouthed and unsure of himself as he waited for the women to seat themselves before he began. Holding onto the back of a kitchen chair for support he began and looked straight at Tiffany.

"I would like to apologize for every mean thing I ever said or did to you. It was wrong and I shouldn't have done it. I hope you can forgive me and we can eventually become friends. I realize trust is earned, and I would like to earn yours if you will let me." Todd balanced himself from foot to foot as he waited for Tiffany's reply. Temperance smiled and elbowed Tiffany in the shoulder to give her a nudge.

"Uhm, thank you, Todd." Tiffany swallowed and looked at Dorothy as if she could not believe her ears. "This is all so very surprising. I'm not sure if I can take it all in. Coming from you, I'm not sure you can be trusted. You caused Billy and I so many problems it wasn't funny." Tiffany paused to take a breath.

"Tiffany, honey, he's apologizing." Temperance smiled at Todd and then at Dorothy. If her daughter could trust him, she could too. "Let's give him a chance. Heaven knows he could probably use the help himself."

Tiffany glanced up and finally put her hand out to shake on it.

"I hope this means we can start over from scratch. No more problems for you and Billy. I promise." Todd shook.

"All right." Tiffany flashed him a tentative smile while she quickly wiped her hand on her apron. "So what are you doing here?" This was the moment that Dorothy had dreaded and still didn't know how to break it to her Mother. Todd came through with flying colors when he stood as tall as he could and started to smile at Dorothy.

"Miss Adams here has offered me a real paying job doing something that I'm very good at." Todd said with pride. "And I won't let her down."

Dorothy was amazed at the attitude change in Todd. She knew that if she offered him a job where he could excel that he would probably take it, but his pride level in that fact surprised even Dorothy.

"I'm going to be your new Gardener, Mrs. Adams. I promise, tomorrow when I arrive early to start my work, I will look and even smell better."

"You hire him to work in the garden?" Maria asked in amazement.

"My daughter should have phoned ahead and let us know she was coming and what she was doing." Temperance admonished Dorothy with her words and a look. Then she turned back to Todd and noticed the way his pride and stubbornness masked the nervousness that he might lose his precious job.

"What makes you the one for this job?" Temperance asked Todd.

"Ma'am, I am a hard worker and I will not treat you with any disrespect. I love to work with my hands and I'm good at it. I do it at home for my mother." Todd paused and took a breath and Dorothy allowed him the chance to continue.

"I know I have a bad reputation, and that you have no reason to trust me now. I've done some rotten things but Miss Adams here has just given me a chance to show everyone, including myself, that I'm not worthless. I would like to do that. So I'm asking you for your help and trust. Just give me one chance and I promise I won't let you down." Todd was actually begging for a job. Dorothy was very surprised at this change in his mental state.

Temperance sat back and pursed her lips for a moment and then turned to Tiffany. "Would you be able to work comfortably in this house if you knew Todd was out there in the yard?" She asked.

"Todd knows how I feel about him but he has apologized." Tiffany began. "I suppose he deserves a second chance. But if he crosses the line one more time . . . well, then I guess what happens would be up to you, Mrs. Adams. But I am willing to give him a chance." Tiffany had just a ghost of a smile on her face. Trying to look stern and disapproving just wasn't possible for a girl with such a sunny personality.

"All right, Maria?" Temperance turned her attention to Maria and what she had to say. Todd sat carefully with his head down. Maria raised her chin and spoke to him.

"You look at me, please, Todd." Todd looked up at the woman who represented the last hurdle to being blessed with his job and what he saw almost made him swallow his tongue.

"You ever hurt any of my family again I will use more than a frying pan on you, do you understand?" Todd nodded. "These people are my family. I grew with them and they are important to me. Anyone tries to hurt them and I will be very angry. That Uncle of yours had better mind his manners too, or I will use my frying pan on him." To emphasize her words, she waved the huge wooden spoon stained with red sauce she still had in her hand. Todd closed his eyes silently in prayer and opened them again and nodded.

"I guess that closes the deal." Temperance began a tentative smile. "Todd Belknap, you are hired. But first, would you mind going home and having a shower?" Todd's excitement made him bounce out of his chair and hug Temperance. Stepping back from her chair he had an open mouthed expression on his face.

"I am so sorry Mrs. Adams. It won't happen again. I won't ever touch you again, I swear!" Temperance started to laugh out loud.

"I don't mind the hug, Todd, but please, have a shower." Everyone around the table was smiling and laughing as Todd rushed to the door. He turned and looked back at the table where the four women sat who told him they knew he was worthy of his trust. Almost overwhelmed with an emotion he couldn't name he spoke once more.

"I am going to go home, Mrs. Adams, and I will get cleaned up. I know it's late, but if you will permit me to I would like to come back and find out where all my tools and equipment are and what remains to be done for the day." Todd held his breath.

"That will be fine, Todd." Temperance nodded approval.

"And Miss Dorothy?" Todd asked.

"Yes, Todd?" she asked.

"Thank you for this chance." He left and closed the door quietly behind him.

Temperance looked directly at Dorothy who tried to hide behind her coffee cup.

"You could have called and warned us." She said in disapproval.

"True. True." Dorothy nodded. "But there just didn't seem to be time." Dorothy then told the ladies around the table about how Todd had called when she was talking to Chief Barns and the surprising turn of events that had transpired at breakfast with Todd.

"You mean he actually saw Therese?" Temperance asked with a puzzled look. Then she isn't in any trouble?"

"Well, Chief Barns didn't say. He just left the table in one heck of a hurry but he did say he would be in touch with us just as soon as he could."

"Will wonders never cease?" Tiffany said with a smile as she stood up. "Here everyone was worried about her being missing and now she has been found. Well, I had better get back to cleaning. I'm upstairs at this moment Mrs. Adams, but I will try to answer the door when the bell rings." She said as she pushed the chair in to the table she had been sitting in.

"Tiffany, you are not a maid. I'm sure whoever is the closest to the door at the time the bell rings will answer it. You have enough to do with this large mansion." Temperance smiled at her enthusiasm.

"Okay, thank you ma'am." Tiffany left the kitchen.

"Me too. I have lasagna to put in the oven." Maria smiled as she went back to the stove and started to hum to herself.

"I am going to the office and work on some of the files your father wanted put in storage." Temperance said. Dorothy stood to join her.

"I'll help. It would do me good to see some of those files so I can get the lay of the land." Dorothy said as they left the room. The smell of lasagna began to waft through the house as well as Maria's voice raised in song.

CHAPTER TWENTY-ONE

By the time Chief Barns got to the office, Elva was pouring him a cup of coffee and she handed it to him as he sat behind his desk. He had come in the back door which was right next to his office door and even though it was in the back of the building, Elva seemed to have a knack for knowing when he was there.

"You have someone waiting to see you in the front waiting room, sir." Elva was strictly business as she waited for Chief Barns to tell her his instructions.

"Who is it?" he asked as he settled in and took a sip of some great tasting coffee. Humor restored he looked up to Elva.

"It's Darien Belknap." Elva said. "He wants to swear out a warrant for the arrest for the person who broke into his car this morning." Chief Barns looked at her with surprise in his eyes.

"Why me? Can't one of the other officers available take his statement?" He lowered his cup.

"No sir. He wants to speak with you personally. He said it has something to do with your investigation into the death of Mr. Adams."

Barns sighed and took another sip of coffee.

"Okay, give me five minutes then . . ." Belknap waltzed right in the door with a superior attitude and an ugly look on his face interrupting Chief Barns. Elva backed out of the door and closed it behind her as she went back to her desk.

"I have been kept waiting for over an hour and I do not like that one bit. I am not some bum from off the street. I am a barrister and solicitor and I do not deserve treatment like this." He plopped himself down in the leather chair across the desk and looked angrily at Chief Barns. Chief Barns matched his angry stare and calmly took another sip of his coffee.

"I have been very busy this morning. If you didn't want to be kept waiting you should have talked to one of my officers." He quietly stated to the man across from him.

"I will not deal with one of your officers. I will only deal with you." Belknap said with stubbornness.

"And that is exactly why you were kept waiting." Barns said and sat back. "Now what is it that couldn't be handled by one of my officers?"

"I had someone break into my car this morning and witnesses will say it was that upstart Dorothy Adams." Belknap had leant forward and tapped the edge of the desk top.

"Really?" Barns scratched the back of his head then reached for a pen. "All right, start from the beginning."

"I was in my office and I always park behind the building in the lot when I heard some glass smashing. I looked out my window and saw her going through the driver's window and she went through my car. By the time I got out to the lot, she had roared off on her bike with my stereo and whatever cash I had in the glove box."

"And what time was this?" Chief Barns asked. He knew that a report had come in that the compound behind the Adams gas station had been broken into this morning as well. He looked up and paused in his writing as Belknap searched his memory.

"It was at precisely 10:34 am." Belknap sat back with a smug smile on his face.

"You're sure it was her?" Chief Barns asked.

"Yes of course. Who else rides a fire truck red motorbike?"

"Was she wearing her helmet? The one that matches her bike?" Barns started writing again with a little smile. If Belknap only knew what was going to hit him in the next few seconds he wouldn't be sitting there with that smug little look on his face.

"Yes! How many times do I have to repeat myself?" Belknap said in exasperation.

All trace of amusement disappeared from Chief Barns' face as he pointed his finger at Belknap in anger. "You listen here. What you are accusing Miss Adams of is a serious accusation and I need you to be absolutely certain of all the details, big or small." He had raised his voice and Belknap began to realize he was not in friendly territory.

"All right, all right! She was wearing that leather outfit with the helmet that covers her whole face and riding her motorbike. That was how she managed to get away so fast."

"That's better." Chief Barns finished writing this down and then pressed the intercom to summon Elva. "Elva, could you bring me the printout of the morning reports, please?" he said into the com.

"Well aren't you going to go out and arrest her?" Belknap demanded.

"No, Darien, I'm not. I am going to write up your report and give it the attention it deserves and then I am going to tell you a thing or two about jumping to conclusions."

"Just what in the hell do you mean by that?" Belknap began to puff up with anger and his face began to get red. Elva chose that moment to walk in with the requested reports and withdraw as quickly as she could.

"In these reports is the mention of a burglary to the compound behind the Adams family gas station. The bike, helmet, and trailer it pulls were all stolen."

"It could still be her! She could have broken in herself!" Belknap struggled to find a logical explanation.

"No she couldn't have done that. Better yet, why would she break in to steal her own bike?"

"I don't know what goes on in the minds of criminals like her. I want you to go out and arrest her right now!"

"I don't give a shit what you want Darien. I will not arrest anyone without positive proof. Hearsay is not proof!" Chief Barns sat back and laced his fingers in front of him on the desk.

"Besides, she couldn't have done it."

"And how in the hell do you know that?"

"At the time that you say she was breaking into your car, I was having coffee with her in the kitchen at the Manor and discussing some legal implications on her father's death. So you see, I am her alibi." Chief Barns smiled to himself. He had let Belknap walk right into the trap. And that definitely felt good with a blowhard like Belknap.

Darien Belknap sat blinking his eyes in surprise. Understanding that he had been out of place in accusing Dorothy Adams didn't make him apologize, it just made him angrier.

"Well what are you going to do about my car?" Belknap snapped back to Chief Barns. Barns calmly picked up his pen and began writing again. He talked while he wrote.

"I told you I will give your statement the attention it deserves, but if I were you I would file a report with your insurance company." A silence began to stretch as Belknap was suddenly unsure of what to do next. Barns looked up.

"Are you still here?" He asked in annoyance. "You can go now." Belknap did not appreciate being dismissed like the unimportant blowhard he was and he showed his displeasure as he made his way to the front door. A verbal tirade followed him all the way.

"*Oh man, was that sweet!*" Chief Barns said to himself with a smile. He laced his fingers behind his head and sat back with his feet up on the corner of the desk. He was in that position when Elva came in with a smile on her face as well.

"Is everything okay in here?" she asked.

"Elva, my dear. Everything is perfect at this moment in time." He laughed. "It isn't every day a person gets to best someone like Darien Belknap." He put his feet down under his desk and began to tell Elva just how fun his conversation with Belknap had been.

CHAPTER TWENTY-TWO

After Belknap left his office Chief Barns received a call from a former officer about the background check on the missing housekeeper. He talked for almost half an hour and when he hung up he sat back in surprise and blew out a deep breath.

"Well, this explains a few things." He said to himself. He summoned Elva to his office and waited for her to enter then motioned for her to close the door.

"What's up, Chief?" Elva asked. "Why all the secrecy?"

"Elva, I need you to do me a favor. Can you please call all the officers on patrol and tell them to keep on the lookout for this Therese, the housekeeper, or former housekeeper at the Manor?" He requested.

"Sure." She answered.

"Plus, I want you to have a patrol car go by the Manor at least once every hour and be on the lookout for anything suspicious."

"Do you want them to know why?" Elva asked.

"Yes, definitely. The former housekeeper happens to be the sister of the girl who passed away in the car crash that Dorothy Adams was involved in fifteen years ago. It took a lot of digging, but after the family moved away, the younger sister blamed Dorothy for the death of her sister and swore she would get even some day." Chief Barns explained. "After she graduated, she changed her looks, changed her name, and came back to Redwood as a housekeeper after the previous one passed away in another car accident. She had access to Mr. Adam's medication, she gained their trust and worked for them for five years in order to get close to Dorothy. I also believe she is responsible for the death of the previous housekeeper. So she is to be reported as dangerous, is that clear?" He looked up to Elva.

"Holy shit, Chief. This stuff only happens in mystery thrillers and television shows. Never in Redwood." Elva could hardly believe her ears.

"Well it has happened here. And we are going to make sure it doesn't happen again. I need to hold a press conference so that I can finally pass out the news that Dorothy Adams was not the one responsible for the accident. That should slow down our little murderess." Chief Barns said.

"Okay, full court?" Elva was suddenly all business as she realized the urgency of the situation.

"Definitely. Can you do that for me?"

"Yes sir. Right away." Elva turned to leave.

"Oh, and Elva, I will call the Adams and go out there myself. I need to explain to them just what is going on so they don't hear it over the news."

"Will do, boss. How does five o'clock sound for the press conference?"

"Perfect, I should be back by then." Barns waved Elva off and reached for the phone.

Dorothy answered the phone and was surprised to hear Chief Barns' voice again so soon. When he told her he had urgent news to tell the whole family, Dorothy suggested he come over immediately. After she hung up, she reached for the phone again and got in contact with the other family members to let them know about the meeting. Then she went in search of her mother.

Walking into the kitchen, Dorothy found Tiffany and Maria having an afternoon tea at the table.

"Have either of you seen mother in the last couple hours?" Dorothy asked.

"Ci!" Maria offered. "She went shopping. She say she needs the break."

"Why, Miss Dorothy? Is something wrong?" Tiffany inquired.

"Well, Chief Barns is on his way over to give us some news and he kind of wanted everyone to be here. I had better give mother a call on her cell." Dorothy walked back to the office and tried to call her mother's cell phone. The voice mail answered immediately and Dorothy cursed her mother's reluctance to use the phone for anything other than emergencies. This was an emergency and she couldn't get in touch with her mother. Just as she finished leaving a message, the door chimes rang and she made her way to the door.

The first of the family members to arrive, Matt and Brenda walked in without their children who were at their sitter's. Chief Barns walked in just after the last family member and they all filed into the living room where everyone could be more comfortable.

"Dorothy, could you please ask Maria and Tiffany to attend this meeting as well?" Barns didn't even notice he used Dorothy's first name. Neither did Dorothy.

"Is Mrs. Adams going to join us?" He inquired.

"She went shopping and she didn't turn her cell phone on so I couldn't reach her. I left her a voice mail to call home as soon as she could." Dorothy answered.

"My goodness! What is going on with all this urgency?" Patricia spoke up from the couch where she sat beside her husband Mark.

Chief Barns cleared his throat and stood in front of the fireplace so he could address everyone at once.

"I did a background check on the former housekeeper you called Therese. It seems she was formerly called Anna. Anna Price." Dorothy was stunned when she heard the name.

"Anna! My god it's been so long. She's changed." Murmurs of agreement were heard around the room.

"All right, this is important so please don't interrupt until I'm finished." Everyone nodded and the Chief talked on. Gasps of surprise and shock were on everyone's faces as the urgency of the situation was finally realized by all.

"We have to find Mother. She's out there on her own." Dorothy's frightened eyes swept the room. Matt stood and went to her side.

"It's okay, sis. We know her favorite shopping haunts and we'll find her." He assured Dorothy.

"I want you to give me a list of places where she would go and from now on, I don't want any one of you to go anywhere alone. I have patrols going by the Manor every hour. It will be this way until Anna is caught. I mean it!" The Chief's stern voice echoed in everyone's ears as he turned to leave.

"I have a press conference to give and I need to get there. One more thing, "he said as he turned, "There is evidence that suggests that Dorothy here, was not the one driving the car the night the accident happened. I am going to announce that at the press conference to try to stall Miss Price in her tracks. Maybe it helps maybe it doesn't." With that announcement he left and showed himself out. Dorothy stood in amazement at the official acknowledgement of her innocence. Now everyone would know that what she claimed happened was the truth. The family gathered around her and congratulated her briefly but Dorothy tried to shake them off.

"Listen, we have to find Mom." They broke up into teams of two, with Dorothy remaining at the Manor with Maria and Tiffany. They were going to keep in contact with their cell phones.

Maria went to the kitchen to busy herself making soup and sandwiches for dinner. She felt the family would need them. Tiffany went to help her while Dorothy sat in the office and kept trying her mother's cell phone. It kept going to voice mail.

One by one, the family teams called in to report not being able to find her. The Chief called Dorothy and told her to turn on her television so she could see the news conference.

Tiffany and Maria sat beside her on the couch and they waited for the news. The program ended and the news began with a correspondent standing in front of a gathering crowd at the steps of city hall. Chief Barns cleared his throat and began his little speech. News reporters recorded, wrote their notes, and scrambled to find a good vantage point. Barns was almost finished when one of the cameras panned the entire crowd and Tiffany squealed as she pointed to two women standing alone at the outskirts of the crowd. They both had floppy sun hats on and one of them stood tall and regal with a very worried look on her face. Dorothy froze as she saw the woman standing so close behind her mother. It was Therese, or Anna Price.

"Oh god no!" Dorothy jumped from her spot on the couch and ran for the phone in the office. Maria screamed and began crossing herself then praying in Spanish. Tiffany held Maria close while Dorothy called her mother's cell phone again.

"Still voice mail!" Dorothy choked. "I'll call Barns' cell. He should be able to catch her." Scrambling to find the number written down somewhere on the desk, the phone rang on its own.

"Dorothy, it's Matt. Did you see the press conference?" He didn't wait for Dorothy to answer. His voice was low and urgent. "I saw them. I am following them. I need help. Call everyone! Call 911. I don't know how long I can stay unseen."

"Okay, Matt. Please! Bring mother home." Dorothy choked. She hung up and called 911, explaining what was happening. The operator told Dorothy they had someone on it and that she should stay home to wait for news instead of rushing out to help. She would only get in the way.

Dorothy said yes and went back out into the front room. The conference was over and the podium was empty. Maria was rocking back and forth still praying while holding her rosary. Tiffany sat silently crying into her handkerchief. Dorothy told the two ladies what was happening and continued to pace back and forth in front of the blank television, waiting for the phone to ring.

All of a sudden there was a crash as the front door was flung open by Brent and Rosie. They flew into the living room, hoping for news of their mother's safe return. When they were told about Matt and Brenda following the two ladies, Brent was ready to run out and help. Dorothy had to restrain him so he wouldn't go flying out the door.

"No Brent. The police officer said we were to stay here and not get in the middle of it. They were following her. Matt is there. He'll make sure mother is safe." Mere seconds after Dorothy said that, the phone rang again.

"Dorothy, Chief Barns." Came the clipped voice. "We've got her. We've got your mother. She's safe. Thanks to Matt." His voice carried a note of relief in it. Dorothy told the news to the whole room. A cheer went up. "We didn't catch Anna, though, she's still out there. I'll explain more when we get Mrs. Adams home." He hung up his cell and didn't give Dorothy a chance to say anything. It wouldn't have mattered anyhow. Dorothy couldn't find the words.

Brent called everyone else in the family that hadn't made it home and the entire family was there when Matt, Brenda, and Temperance were driven up in a patrol car. Chief Barns himself opened the back door of the squad car and assisted Temperance out of the back, followed by Matt and Brenda. No one waited for them to come up the steps. The family flew down the steps to embrace their mother and make sure she really was okay, including Tiffany and Maria.

"All right, all right. Let's let them get inside before they fall over from fatigue." Chief Barns urged everyone back up the steps. He turned back and gave his officers in the second car instructions and they got out and began to circle around to the back yard. Back inside, they had Temperance seated at the kitchen table with a hot cup of tea and everyone stood or sat around her, waiting to hear what happened.

""You take your time, Mother. When you are ready, you can tell us what happened." Dorothy put her arms around her mother's shoulder in concern. Temperance tapped her hand with her own.

"It's okay, dear. I'm fine. But I am not one to waste such a fine cup of tea when I need it so much." She reached out and took a sip, closing her eyes. As she did this a silence descended on the entire room. "Ah, that's better. Now, where should I start?"

Temperance started with getting to the clothing store and having a funny feeling that someone was watching her. She kept looking over her shoulder but couldn't see anyone. Then she went to the grocery store for a few things when Anna came up behind her and forced her to go along with her to the car.

"She said she had a gun and she would use it." Temperance's voice wavered for a moment so she took another sip of tea. Smoothing her hair back behind her right ear she composed herself enough to go on. "We went to the car and when I started it, she got into the passenger seat in the front and made me wear that floppy sun hat. I tried to ask her why she was doing that when an announcement about a news conference came on the radio. Well all of a sudden, she had me change direction and we parked behind City Hall in a towing zone and went to hear the conference. She warned me she would use the gun if I didn't do what she told me. Well I wasn't going to argue with her." Temperance paused for another sip of her tea. "When Chief Barns explained about the mix up in information at the car accident fifteen years ago and that there was new information that Dorothy was innocent, well, that girl started swearing a blue streak. She didn't believe Chief Barns and she pulled me with her to try to get back to the car. Thank goodness Matt was following with Brenda. If they hadn't been there, I don't know what I would have done." Temperance reached out and took Matt's hands in hers and kissed them then held them to her cheek. Tears of love appeared in Temperance's eyes and she couldn't go on.

"Brenda and I followed them back to where they had parked the car, only it had been towed. She started looking around for some other means of transportation when she saw me and Brenda. I thought for sure she was going to fire her gun, but for some strange reason she didn't" Matt was crying as well and couldn't finish over the lump in his throat.

"What happened next was Mrs. Adams told Anna she forgave her and elbowed her in the gut then ran like hell." Chief Barns picked up the story. "Two officers of mine had spotted the two ladies and realized the situation and they moved in, causing Anna Price to back up and run in the other direction. They lost her in the alley. By the time they came back to where your Mother and Matt and Brenda were, Matt and Brenda could not be separated from your mother so we brought them all home. Safe." Maria crossed herself and Tiffany hugged her for support.

"Thank you Chief Barns." Dorothy looked him in the eyes. "You don't know how much this means to us." Dorothy held out her hand to shake. Her gut began to cramp and her toes began to curl again as the Chief looked directly into her eyes. He hesitated and instead of shaking hands, he reached out, took her shoulders in his very large and warm hands, pulled her closer, and kissed her on the forehead. Releasing her gently he backed up and turned away with a smile.

"I think I do." He said more to himself as he helped himself to a cup of coffee. Maria began crossing herself all over again.

CHAPTER TWENTY-THREE

It was a little while before emotions around the table began to settle down. Maria served soup and sandwiches, and Tiffany made sure all the coffee cups were full. All the talk was about how proud they were that Dorothy's name had been cleared and Temperance was safe. Chief Barns received a phone call and then turned to leave.

"I want you all to understand, Anna Price is still out there. We don't know where, but we just received a lead and I have to go. Do not go anywhere on your own again Mrs. Adams. Not until we have her in jail where she belongs. Understand?" Temperance nodded and agreed. Barns nodded his head to Dorothy in goodbye and Maria and Tiffany began to smile at each other. Dorothy escorted him to the door and with each step she could feel the touch of his warm, soothing lips on her forehead. Her gut was still clenched as well.

"I will see you tomorrow as soon as I can. The Patrols have been set to pass by every hour. That's the best I can do." Chief Barns said as he went out the door. Dorothy stood and watched him leave and gave a little wave. Her confusion seemed to take over her completely and she jumped when Matt came up behind her unnoticed.

"Hey little sister. You seemed pretty chummy with Chief Barns, there. Anything we should know?"

"Huh? Aahh, no. Nothing." She stammered as she looked up at Matt. Matt almost laughed when he saw her eyes. She was stunned.

"That's okay, little sister. Let's go back to the table and finish our conversation." Matt put his arm around Dorothy and led her back towards the kitchen. *I think Dorothy has just been bitten by the love bug.* He smiled to himself.

CHAPTER TWENTY-FOUR

The next morning brought sun and a cool breeze and the feeling for Dorothy that everything was finally all right with the world. Her world, anyhow. She had a quiet breakfast with her mother and decided to work from home instead of running around the city. It would be safer for her mother, anyhow.

Maria and Tiffany were happily going about their jobs when Todd showed up clean shaven, smiling, and in a pair of coveralls. Dorothy discussed the details of how she wanted the gardens to look like, what needed to be done, and how she wanted the grass cut.

"Are you sure you know where all the tools are?" Dorothy quizzed him as he stood in the entrance off the kitchen.

"Yes ma'am. Maria was kind enough to show me where the shed was and she even gave me the key. I should get started now so I can mow the lawn before the sprinklers kick in. Have a good day, ma'am." Todd was gone to the yard with a nod and a smile and Dorothy shook her head in amazement.

"What a difference in attitude." Dorothy thought to herself. "All he needed was someone to like him and show him a little trust. I think he has been waiting for this for a long time." Dorothy thanked Maria for the wonderful breakfast and went into the office.

It wasn't long before she had the files rearranged the way she liked them so she could access them. The time was close to lunch by then and Dorothy was going to go in search for a coffee when the phone on the desk rang.

"Hello, Dorothy speaking."

"Hey there, Dorothy. Trevor here. I found the information you wanted on Jim Marshall." Dorothy sat back down and leaned back in the chair.

"Thank you Trevor. I hope its good news." Dorothy began to feel some tension around her neck and started to rub the back of it.

"Depending on how you look at it, yeah, I think it is. At least you'll know what you are facing." Came the matter of fact voice.

"Okay, Trevor, let's have it." She said. The sun shining in the window that gave her such a good feeling minutes before, now went unnoticed as Dorothy concentrated on what Trevor had to say.

"First of all, Jim Marshall has impeccable references. He has been a lawyer all his adult life, graduated law school in Toronto, passed the bar there, and came out here in search of a quiet, but expensive life style. It seems he has succeeded in doing so. His business dealings began to get a little fudgy around five years ago, when he went into a real estate investment scheme with Darien Belknap." Dorothy's heart rate picked up when she heard Darien's name.

"The two of them lost their shirts on that and Darien declared bankruptcy. But get this, there was another investor involved from Toronto and he wasn't too happy to lose all his money."

"Who was the investor?" Dorothy asked.

"Quentin Tallas." Dorothy was stunned at the answer.

"*The* Quentin Tallas?" she blurted out. "The real estate mogul of Toronto, no one makes a move in real estate without his say so Quentin Tallas?"

"That's the one." Trevor answered. "Apparently, he is pushing the two of them to come up with some cash or he will take over the family business which your father apparently signed over to Jim Marshall."

"Oh really. My father signed over the business that he had built to Jim Marshall." Dorothy's disbelief showed plainly on her face and in her voice.

"I have a copy of the document in question if you should so like it." Trevor smiled into the phone. Dorothy liked the way her former lieutenant was still able to read her mind.

"You send me the document and I will send *you* a sample of my father's hand writing." Dorothy suggested. "That way you can check to see if the handwriting on the signature is really my father's."

"All right." Trevor acknowledged the request. "I will get on that immediately as soon as you get me that sample."

"Is there anything else I should know about?" Dorothy asked.

"Just that I will be sending you all the information and you should get it by tomorrow." Trevor once again smiled into the phone. "What I wouldn't give to be a fly on the wall when you have your meeting with

Jim Marshall." Trevor laughed. "Should I send you a copy of his bank statement?"

"Do I want a copy of his bank statement?" Dorothy asked.

"Oh yes, you definitely do." Trevor answered. "That way you will know how much Jim Marshall owes your family."

"All right, send it as soon as possible." Dorothy answered as the anger at Jim Marshall began to build.

"Done." Trevor said. Dorothy's smart phone on the desk began to vibrate and ring. Picking it up she saw a message from Trevor.

"Very fast, Trevor. You just might make some money at this security stuff someday." Trevor hung up with a chuckle.

Dorothy spent several minutes sending the message to her desk top and printing out the information she received. She was astounded at what she read and angered even more by the antics of Darien Belknap but more so because of Jim Marshall's complicity. She went to find her mother so they could discuss what the next step should be.

Temperance was in the library, busy using her sewing machine in the corner. She looked up as Dorothy entered with a knock and a smile.

"Hello Mother. Still sewing those quilts?" She asked as she approached. Temperance had always been good at sewing quilts, and had made it a very profitable past time for herself. Dorothy's father had acknowledged that ability with pride as he deliberately made a corner of the library a little work area for Temperance. When Temperance looked up and saw the look on Dorothy's face she sat back and turned off the sewing machine.

"What's wrong Dorothy?" she asked.

"I just got off the phone with a friend of mine and he gave me some information on our friend and family lawyer, Jim Marshall." Temperance's brow furled in anxiety.

"It's not good, is it?" She surmised.

"No, mother, it isn't. I think we need to have a meeting with the family and Chief Barns to decide how we are going to handle the matter." A slight tremor at the corner of Temperance's mouth appeared as she struggled to keep a smile from her face.

"Why do we need Chief Barns?" Temperance inquired with a sparkle in her eye. Dorothy noticed it and pursed her lips.

"It's a serious matter. We need some advice on how to proceed legally and have things straightened out. It is not a matter for your amusement."

Dorothy said sternly, annoyed her mother and everyone else seemed to get that same look on their face when she mentioned Chief Barns.

"Okay. Let's do it." Temperance couldn't quite wipe the smile from her face. Just then, the house phone rang and her mother reached over and picked it up from the desk.

"Adams residence." She said. The glint in her eyes became more pronounced as she handed the phone to Dorothy. "Speak of the devil . . ." her voice trailed off as Dorothy took the phone in exasperation.

"Hello." She snapped into the phone. "Dorothy here."

"Miss Adams," Chief Barns paused in surprise at the annoyance in her tone. "I was hoping we could have a meeting this morning to talk about some information that just passed over my desk from an outside source. It has an important bearing on your father's case. Could you come in as soon as possible?"

"Will it be an interrogation or just a meeting?" Dorothy barked, still annoyed. Temperance smiled as she stood and left the sewing table and went to the desk to listen to the one sided conversation.

"Aah, a meeting." Chief Barns paused again. "Did I interrupt something?"

"No, not at all Chief Barns." Dorothy's cool voice came back over the phone. "My mother and I were just discussing our next course of action. And I will be happy to come to your office for a meeting." Dorothy's stubborn chin stuck out and she rubbed the back of her neck in a nervous gesture.

"All right. I'll even put on some fresh coffee." Chief Barns rang off and sat back in amusement. 'I wonder what they were talking about when I interrupted.' A grin suddenly split his handsome face from ear to ear. Reaching for the com he asked Elva to check for fresh coffee and fresh donuts for his meeting.

Out at the front desk, Elva turned to the officer sitting at the desk next to hers.

"I wonder who the meeting is with. He never asks for fresh coffee or donuts when he has a meeting with us." The other officer answered with a silent smile and went back to his file. Elva shrugged and set out for the donut shop next door.

CHAPTER TWENTY-FIVE

Dorothy was ushered into Chief Barn's office half an hour later by a very curious Elva. She left and closed the door behind her after nodding to Chief Barns. On her way to the coffee nook she started to smile. Now she knew why Chief Barns was making the extra effort to have this meeting seem comfortable. It was nice to see Chief Barns was actually getting out into the social circle again. It made him such a nice boss to work for.

In his office, Chief Barns motioned for Dorothy to be seated and sat back in his seat then cleared his throat.

"Thank you for coming in this morning. I've asked Elva, the receptionist to bring us coffee and donuts, if you don't mind." He stated. His mood was light and his face showed nothing of the seriousness of the situation they were about to discuss. Just being able to look at Dorothy, even when she appeared suspicious, gave a little tug on his heart. Her petite frame, auburn colored hair, and blue eyes made his stomach seem to clench in a nice way whenever he saw her lately. Even in grave situations such as this.

"Did you order Boston Cream?" Dorothy asked in a voice so innocent Barns was instantly on the alert.

"Boston Cream? I think so. Why? Does it matter?" He asked.

"I will not talk business without Boston Cream. That's a deal breaker." The smile appeared instantly on her face and they both laughed together as Elva came back in with a tray of coffee and donuts.

The little joke seemed to lighten the atmosphere for Dorothy as well. Elva left the office again with a hum and a big smile.

Once the door closed behind Elva, Chief Barns served the coffee and then got down to business.

"Miss Adams, I have just received some information I think has a bearing on your father's case, as I've said before." Barns began.

"Dorothy. My name is Dorothy, please. Miss Adams sounds so formal after everything that has happened lately." Dorothy couldn't help smiling. In her head she heard '*What the hell am I doing?*'

"Thank you Dorothy. Please call me Ethan." Dorothy nodded with a smile and in his head, Chief Barns heard '*What the hell am I doing?*'

"I heard that your family lawyer, James W. Marshall, has had some questionable land investments that he lost his shirt on." Barns became all business.

"Yes, so have I." Dorothy nodded again. "My source told me he also is in league with an out of town real estate developer Quentin Tallas and Darien Belknap." Ethan looked at Dorothy in surprise.

"You have very good sources, Dorothy. May I ask who your source is?"

"You can ask but I won't tell you." Dorothy leaned forward and handed her cell phone over to Ethan. "I have pulled up some documents sent to me and they show bank statements, a bogus document giving Jim Marshall permission to do what he wanted with the funds in our business account, and I am expecting confirmation on the fraudulent signature at the bottom of that document." Ethan viewed the information on the smartphone and was silent while he digested its significance.

"I can see we are going to have to have a talk with Mr. Marshall and Mr. Belknap. As for this Quentin Tallas fellow, can you give me some background on him?"

Dorothy explained the complicated relationship on Quentin Tallas and the other two men in question. She also informed Ethan about Tallas' other investments and financial dealings in Toronto.

"So you don't think he would have anything to do with your father's death?" Ethan asked her opinion.

"No. I think my father's death was actually inconvenient for him and he had nothing to do with it. With my father alive, he could actually go after him legally to recover funds he lost in his dealings with Belknap and Marshall. Now that my father is dead, he has to wait for the will to be executed legally, before he can place any claims against it. I believe Belknap and Marshall are the ones who are trying to create problems for us financially in order to force us to sell at a reduced asking price. My father's death I believe is the result of a seriously misguided young lady who probably still believes I am the reason she lost her sister in that car crash." Ethan listened and heard the logical reasoning behind her ideas.

"I think you're right about that. And so, we now have to figure out what you would like to do about Belknap and Marshall." Ethan stated.

"Is there anything I can do legally?" Dorothy asked. "Is there enough evidence against the two of them yet?"

"Not yet. And the evidence you have here will have to be obtained through official channels. A warrant can be obtained to search Marshal's office for fraud and hopefully it will lead us to his connection to Belknap. But if we produce a warrant, Marshall will know we are looking at him and he will flee. So I want to hold off a little longer on that score. Can your family handle that?" He asked Dorothy.

"Of course. It's not a problem. I have an idea on how to handle Quentin Tallas in Toronto without causing any problems for the investigation." Dorothy nodded.

"Have you had any communication or sightings of Anna Price?" Ethan asked next.

"None. But I have hired young Todd Belknap to do the yard work. I could ask him if he's seen anything." Dorothy inquired.

Ethan smiled in surprise again. "Young Todd Belknap?" Ethan queried. "How did you manage that? And do you trust him."

"It will take some getting used to, but I saw something of myself in Todd and asked him if he wanted a job. He jumped at the chance to help instead of hinder." Dorothy smiled. "Don't look so surprised. He's showered, shaved, no longer has his Mohawk hair style and wears a pair of coveralls instead of black leather studded belts and army boots." Ethan started to laugh softly.

"I guess I am no longer surprised at anything you do." Ethan smiled gently at Dorothy and the two of them sat there for a moment too long, gazing into each other's eyes. The com beside the phone on the desk buzzed and they both jumped guiltily.

"Yes, Elva?" Ethan talked into the com.

"There has been a report of another break and enter at the Adams compound behind their service station. I thought you might want to check it out right away." Elva's voice was all business.

"Yes I do. Thank you Elva." Ethan Barns, Chief of Police reached for his hat and placing it on his head, looked at Dorothy as he stood.

"Would you like to accompany me to the compound?" He motioned towards the door.

"No, that's fine. I'll drive over there myself." Dorothy answered. They both left the office at the same time and went to their vehicles.

Dorothy sat in her car for a moment as Chief Barns roared off in his with the siren blazing. Looking up at the ceiling of the car she cleared her throat.

"I know everything happens for a reason. And always at the time it was meant to happen. But you are confusing me, God. Am I supposed to like or love this Ethan Barns? It scares the hell out of me to think I am beginning to trust him a little more every time I see him." Dorothy let out a big sigh and reached forward to turn the key. "*I sure hope you know what you are doing.*" She muttered to herself as she backed out of her spot.

She pulled in behind Chief Barns' car at the service station. As she did so, Billy came running out to her with distress written all over his face.

"Aunt Dorothy, I am so sorry." Billy seemed to be at the point of tears. "She took your bike and now she returned it. I am so sorry for what she did to it." Dorothy gave Billy a friendly pat on the shoulder to comfort him.

"It's okay, Billy. I knew about the theft but I am happy someone returned it." She began to smile. Billy took a couple steps backward and shook his head.

"You won't be when you see it." He warned her. Matt came bounding out of the service station with an unpleasant look on his face.

"Billy, I want you to attend to the customers in the front while I take Dorothy to the back to see what has happened." Matt instructed his son in a harsh voice. Billy looked down in with a hurt expression on his face.

"Yes, Dad." He went to the pumps to help the customer that had just pulled up. Matt took Dorothy's elbow and walked her through the front office and into the back of the bay. They went through the back door and came out into the sunshine where Dorothy could see the smashed gate of the chain link fence which surrounded the compound. She shielded her eyes so she could see better and gasped at the wanton destruction displayed in front of her.

The motorcycle she had ridden into town on was spread out on the ground in little pieces. It had been totally dismantled and thrown around the yard. The trailer had been hacked to pieces with a hatchet and the canvas top had been cut into tiny little pieces. Chief Barns looked up when he heard Dorothy's gasp and came towards them. Matt held firmly to her elbow so Dorothy couldn't run forward to her bike. Or what was left of it.

"Oh my God!" Dorothy breathed out in shock. "Why would she do that?"

Ethan joined the two of them and shrugged at his perplexity. "I guess this proves she is still determined that you are responsible for what happened all those years ago." He reached out and gently touched Dorothy's other elbow to comfort her. Matt noticed the gesture and struggled to keep the smile from his face.

"I am going to have to ask that you don't go in there until we have collected everything we can in the forensics department." Ethan said gently. "Maybe Matt had better take you home."

"Not before you tell me how she got in here." Dorothy said in anger. "I deserve to know that much."

"Chief! Over here, hurry!" An officer, who had been checking out the wooden foot locker on the ground in the corner of the compound, was motioning frantically at Chief Barns.

Ethan took off running and pulled up short beside the other officer. Looking down into the box his face turned white. Dorothy broke away from Matt and went through the gate before he could catch her. She reached the foot locker just in time to glimpse its contents before the officer slammed the lid shut. Ethan grabbed her above the elbows to hold her back. A buzzing began in Dorothy's head at the sight of Anna Price, all pale and unseeing in death. Matt reached Dorothy's side just as she passed out. Ethan lifted her in his arms and carried her over to the squad car. Matt opened the back seat and Ethan sat her gently inside. Chief Barns stepped back and let Matt tend to her while he called for an ambulance.

"Matt, she's dead. It's Anna and she's dead!" The shock hit Matt as he tried to reassure Dorothy.

Billy came racing around the corner with something shiny in his hand just as Ethan finished calling for the ambulance.

"Dad! Dad!" he said in excitement.

"What, Billy? I thought I told you to stay up front." Matt snapped in annoyance and fear.

"But Dad, I fixed the surveillance camera yesterday and I have the footage on this DVD." He said in a rush.

"Billy, you never told me you fixed that camera." His dad reached for the DVD. Ethan reached out and snatched it out of mid air.

"Thank you Billy. That was a great thing you did. You may have helped us catch a murderer." Ethan stated as he put the disc in a plastic evidence envelope and sealed it.

"Murder?" Billy stammered. "What murder? I thought this was about your bike Aunt Dorothy." Billy suddenly saw the state that Dorothy was in and realized he had walked into a situation he didn't want to be in.

"Billy, I don't want you to say anything to anyone about this. Now run and get Aunt Dorothy some cold water and a cold cloth." Matt urged his son with a little smile of encouragement. Billy left so fast, Dorothy blinked and he was gone.

CHAPTER TWENTY-SIX

The ambulance pulled up and checked Dorothy out to make sure she was okay. All the while they were taking her pulse and other vitals, Matt was instructing Billy about shutting down the pumps early. He could hear Dorothy protesting in the background and he grimaced when he turned to watch.

'All that she has seen and she still faints." He mused to himself. "Little sister, little sister." He said out loud as he walked over to the gurney that Dorothy sat on. "Let them check you out and then I will take you home." Matt assured her.

"I am not your little sister, you are *my* little brother!" She pushed away the hands of the female paramedic in anger. "Leave me alone!" she cried.

"Okay, big sister. You are older than me. But if you don't sit still and let them work on you, I will tell Mom on you." Dorothy glared at Matt and became silent. The grateful paramedics smiled at Matt and went about their duties. Matt looked over at the crime scene as the van from the morgue pulled up and two men stepped out of the van dressed in white coveralls. One went to the back of the van and pulled out a gurney while the other went over to Chief Barns and the other officer. Both Matt and Dorothy watched in silence as the coroner bent over the footlocker. Dorothy shut her eyes but she could still see Anna Price in jeans and a white t-shirt, curled in a fetal position with duct tape over her mouth, wrists, and ankles. She made a little sound of mewling in her throat and Matt instantly turned back to her. Going down on one knee in front of Dorothy he took her hand.

"Its okay, Dot. We're all here. The memory can't hurt you. Not anymore." Matt had guessed correctly about the cause of Dorothy's anguish. She opened her eyes and let the tears flow.

"It was horrible, Matt. She looked so terrified and afraid." Matt held Dorothy and let her cry while the paramedics backed away. Heavy sobs came forth as Dorothy finally let go of her pain and mental anguish.

"Why did she have to die?" She asked as she held on to Matt for dear life. "Why?"

"I don't know, sweetheart." Matt said as he rubbed Dorothy's shoulders with his broad hand. Eventually the sobs subsided and Dorothy sat back on the gurney. Chief Barns approached the gurney warily. His eyes asked the paramedics a silent question and they nodded.

"Dorothy, I am going to have to ask you where you were yesterday around eight in the evening." He cleared his throat.

Dorothy's head shot up and glared at Chief Barns. Tears and mascara stained her cheeks and her eyes were red and blood shot.

"What? Are you asking me for an alibi?" Dorothy yelled at him. To the female paramedic she asked for Kleenex. The paramedic handed her the whole box and backed away in a hurry.

"Dorothy, I know you must think . . . ." Ethan began and Dorothy cut him off before he could finish.

"No you don't know what I think. I didn't kill this girl. I was at home with my mother and Maria." If looks could kill Ethan would have been a goner at that moment. Instead, he stood with his hat in hand and scuffing the toe of his boot into the sand of the parking lot.

"I don't believe you are asking Dorothy that question." Matt said to Ethan in anger. The sun was extremely bright and it glinted off Ethan's sun glasses.

"It's my job, Matt. I also have to know where each member of your family was." Ethan held out his right hand palm up, as if asking for silent understanding.

"What? Now you're pointing the finger at my entire family?" Matt's outrage was very noticeable as the tips of his ears began to get red.

"No, Matt. I am trying to eliminate your family from suspicion. That's all." Ethan put his hat back onto his head.

"Why?" Dorothy stood up off the gurney and stepped up to Ethan. "Why should we have to defend ourselves?" She demanded, looking into the sunglasses. If she had been able to see the misery in Ethan's eyes, she would have understood how hard it was for him to ask the question.

"Dorothy, please. I told you I need to eliminate you from the suspect list. It's for your own protection that I am doing this." His voice pleaded. Dorothy continued to stare at his glasses for a few more seconds then she turned and walked towards her car.

"I'll make sure you get a minute by minute accounting on your desk within the hour." She opened the car door and glanced back angrily at

Ethan and Matt. "Matt, I suggest you do the same." Her car drove away with a swirl of dust and Ethan felt like his heart went with it.

"I will phone the rest of the family and get them to do the same." Matt said as he stood beside Ethan, watching Dorothy's car disappear down the service road.

"Did she seem pissed to you?" Ethan asked Matt. Matt smiled and turned to the side to look at Ethan.

"Naw, you'll know when she's pissed. Right now she's just fighting it." Matt slapped Ethan on his shoulder in a friendly manner.

"Fighting what?" Ethan asked Matt with a curious look on his face. Matt laughed and walked away.

"You'll figure it out." With that, Matt went to the front of the service station and the pumps and helped Billy close down, leaving a confused Ethan scratching the back of his head. The paramedics just smiled and stowed away their gear and left.

CHAPTER TWENTY-SEVEN

Two days later, Chief Barns was going through all the reports on his desk, signing some and reading others. It had been a particularly interesting couple of days. All the alibis of the Adams family had checked out and Ethan had sighed with relief. Officer Harmon had viewed the security footage on the DVD and made a copy for the Chief. The DVD showed a very frantic Darien Belknap pulling up to the compound just as Anna Price finished destroying the bike.

The two of them argued and Darien had snapped, strangling Anna with his bare hands. Then he taped her up and put her in the foot locker. Once he had done that, he had left, never knowing that the broken security camera had been fixed by Billy. Everything had been captured by the camera.

An all points bulletin had been put out for Darien and so far, they had not been able to catch up with him. He had taken his clothes, all the money in his family's joint bank account and left town right after he had strangled Anna Price. No one knew what the argument was about, but it was generally surmised by Ethan and the District Attorney that the two must have known each other in some way. The DA said he believed that Darien blamed all his problems on the fact that Anna Price had brought all his financial fraud out into the open. Darien's wife had no idea where he went and she was devastated by Darien's lack of consideration for her and the children.

"Maybe that's not such a bad thing for his wife that Darien took off." Ethan sighed and signed the report.

The next file held the information on Jim Marshall and his fraud case. Jim had embezzled more than a million dollars from the Adams estate over the last two years. He had covered it up by moving money from one bank account to another. Mr. Adams had been virtually too sick to notice and had left Power of Attorney for paying bills only to Jim Marshall. A document stating just such an arrangement had been found in Jim Marshall's safe in his office. The fake document giving Marshall permission for all matters pertaining to finances had been checked by a handwriting expert. The signature had been certified as fake. Now Jim Marshall was to be brought up on charges, as soon as they could find him. A search had been made of all means of transportation from cars to planes and they had come up empty. Being a widower for over three years now, Marshall had no ties left to the community, and had virtually vanished without a trace.

Ethan sighed as he signed that paper and closed the folder, placing both files in the out box. Looking around the office he tried to think of a reason to call the Manor and see if Dorothy would talk to him. Three times he had called and been told if he wanted to talk to her, he would have to go through her lawyer. Knowing her lawyer had disappeared, he made a call to Matt and had been informed that Dorothy had indeed hired a lawyer who came down from Edmonton to talk to her. He sat back in his chair and began to rub the back of his neck. Ethan couldn't get the last time he had seen her face all tear stained and angry as she walked away.

"*She looked so beautiful.*" He said out loud to himself then shook his head and jumped as Elva came into the room.

"Who did?" she asked.

"No one. You wouldn't know her." Ethan waved his hand as if to change the subject. "What do you need Elva?" Ethan was suddenly all business as he shuffled the papers around on his desk.

"The DA wants to talk to you about new developments on the two cases you have before you." She answered.

"Why doesn't he call me on the phone?" Elva leaned against the door jamb with a 'How the hell should I know' look on her face and shrugged.

"Then please go back to your desk and I will call him." Ethan instructed.

"It's a little late for that. He's waiting in the outer office with a brief case and an angry look on his face." Elva said. She turned and left. Ethan slapped his forehead with his hand. Everyone was acting so strange for the last couple of days.

"Chief Barns, I want to know why you haven't found our two criminals yet." The DA walked in without ceremony and sat in the chair across from the Chief. Ethan looked up in consternation.

"Probably because they are very good at hiding." He answered. The DA looked like he had been slapped in the face.

"I beg your pardon!" the sallow faced man said in indignation.

"Look! I have just signed a report explaining everything and it is here in my out box for you to look at. We had put up road blocks to find the both of them as soon as we knew what was happening, but they had at least a twelve hour head start. Belknap took his car and we have no idea how Marshall left the city. He virtually disappeared into thin air. Now as soon as we have more to go on, you will be the first to know." Ethan slapped his hat on his head and pushed his chair away from his desk as he stood up. Walking around the desk and towards the door he ignored the sputtering man in his office.

"Elva, give our precious DA a donut and send him on his way with a copy of the reports I just signed on my desk, would 'ya?"

"Sure, Chief." Elva answered. Elva smiled to herself. The DA was not a popular man in this office and she really enjoyed it when someone was able to put him in his place. She walked into Ethan's office and saw the DA sitting and staring at the chair Ethan had just vacated with a stunned look on his face.

"He's gone now, sir. You can go too." Elva said in a neutral tone. The DA collected himself and rose to leave. He got as far as the door when Elva held out a tray of donuts. "Chief said you could have one." The man fairly flew out the door with a few guffaws following him from the other officers.

"Well shoot!" Elva said out loud. "If he isn't going to have one, I will." To the rest of the office she said. "Coffee's on!"

CHAPTER TWENTY-EIGHT

Matt was surveying the damage done to the compound gate after the crime scene tape had been taken down. A week had gone by and still there was no word about the capture of either Jim Marshall or Darien Belknap and that worried Matt. If Darien was addlebrained enough to throttle Anna Price with his bare hands, he wasn't above trying to take revenge against the family. Even though it wasn't Dorothy's fault, Matt knew that human nature would dictate either one of those two criminals would probably blame her. The feeling around the city was that it was all Dorothy's fault that this crime wave hit the city. She came home and everything broke loose. Shaking his head to clear it and focus on the job at hand, he picked up the post hole auger and began drilling out a new post hole for the gate. This time it was going to be set in cement so it would be that much more difficult for someone to break in. Matt wiped his brow and frowned as he remembered the call he had received from his insurance agent.

The insurance was going to be paid with a $1,000 deductible. And the rate would go up. At this rate, Matt might have to close the compound to outside customers and just have it for personal and family use. The sun beating down on Matt's massive frame soon had Matt sweating profusely as he finished with the post hole. Just as he was about to mix the cement for the hole to anchor the post, his cell phone rang. He let out a huge sigh of relief for the brief respite.

"Matt here."

"Matt, Chief Barns here. Where are you at right now?" Came the inquisitive voice.

"Digging a post hole in my back compound. Why? What happened now?" Matt's suspicion was evident in his voice.

"Nothing. I was just hoping you and I could have a coffee or iced tea. Your place of choice, and my treat." Ethan said into his phone.

Matt dropped the shovel he was holding and wiped his brow with a large bandanna he produced from his back jeans pocket.

"What's the occasion?" he asked.

"Like I said, Matt. No special occasion. Just an invitation for coffee."

Matt was thinking to himself that it wasn't every day the Chief of Police invites someone out for coffee for no reason.

"Yeah, sure. Meet you at Wendy's just down from the Shell." Matt answered. If there was something going on *he*, Matt Adams was going to find out. "Say, half an hour?"

"Okay, see you there." Ethan closed his cell phone and glanced around him at the traffic. He was sitting at the top of what the local citizens liked to call 'The Loop' and looking at the view. It was breathtaking in every way. Even the recent growth of the city did nothing to hide that original view. He had needed some place to go to think about things and clear his head and Elva had suggested this rest stop. Taking a deep breath he knew what he was breathing in was almost pure oxygen. Or as close to it as a person could get living in the city. In Redwood, he knew he had found his home. The place he had always dreamt about.

Ethan only had one problem in his personal life left unsolved at this point and that was what was consuming most of his mental energy of late. He closed his eyes and pictured Dorothy as he had last seen her, mascara running down her face, eyes all swollen and red from crying over the death of a person who had sworn to hate her, yet still a trace of strength in the anger emanating from her eyes. Dorothy's long auburn hair was matted and messy, hanging in her eyes, and she had dirt all over her t-shirt and jeans, but she was still the most beautiful thing Ethan had ever seen in his life. The strength and the steel that held her together in one of the most traumatic moments of her life had captured his heart at that moment.

Dorothy hadn't called in to the office for the last few days, and Ethan could understand why. Talking to him would only bring back some unpleasant memories for her. Yet he was always on edge, looking around for a reason to call her just to hear her voice over the phone and Ethan knew he couldn't let that continue for much longer. He couldn't concentrate on work, he wasn't eating, and he wasn't sleeping. Perhaps this coffee with Matt would help him figure out a way to find out just exactly how Dorothy felt about him. Opening his eyes he stood and smoothed the wrinkles out of his uniform shirt and headed over to the meeting with Matt.

Dorothy was sitting in the office at the Manor after just having had a conversation with her banker. There was a pleased smile on her face as she leaned back and laced her fingers behind her head. The news she had just received would help alleviate the cash crunch for the family business and it had taken a weight from her shoulders. She had discussed it with her mother before making the decision and Temperance had agreed to the move. It was just so logical, that it had taken a few days for it to come to Dorothy.

It seemed that every time she closed her eyes she saw Ethan in his uniform and mirrored sunglasses. His smile, his cologne, his voice in her head, the familiar crunch in the gut; it was driving her crazy. She couldn't seem to focus on anything for very long. Not having had this feeling before, she really didn't know what it was and she didn't know if she liked it or not. When Dorothy closed her eyes at night she couldn't sleep without seeing him in her dreams. She had noticed her lack of appetite and had decided she had to do something about this mess she was in or she was going to wind up going stark raving mad. That's why she had called Quentin Tallas in Toronto and made the business proposal that sat on her desk.

Temperance was busy in the library with her sewing with a worried look on her face. She had noticed Dorothy's lack of appetite and she was hoping it wasn't because of the financial mess she had to straighten out. With all the things left to be done after Jim Marshall had fled the city, fixing the financial condition of the family business was a monumental undertaking. Temperance wondered if it wasn't too much for Dorothy.

The phone rang in the office and Dorothy answered.

"Adams residence."

"How are you today, Miss Adams?" Came the well modulated and slick voice of Quentin Tallas.

"I'm fine, Quentin." Unlike the way Ethan's voice made her feel good inside, Quentin's made her shiver with dislike. However, letting him know that wouldn't help the deal go through that she had just proposed.

"That's fine, fine. Say listen little lady, I was wondering if there was a nice place to stay for when I come into town to sign the papers for our deal." The oiliness of his voice was annoying to say the least.

"Quentin, you just bought three hotels from me, which one do you want to stay in?" Dorothy tried to keep the sentiment out of her voice.

"I was hoping I would receive an invitation to stay at the most famous home in the city." Dorothy knew he meant he wanted to stay at the Manor and her mouth dropped open in surprise. She knew she would never let a snake like Quentin Tallas in the front door, let alone stay one single minute. The nerve of the man!

"Quentin, may I remind you that we are completing a business deal, and there are no fringe benefits. You have your hotels, and I have my Bed and Breakfast. Period! That's it, there is no more!"

"Well at least you are letting me know where I stand." Quentin mused to himself. "All right, well then I will just tell you that I will arrive in the city tomorrow afternoon, and I would like to make an appointment to see you and sign the papers at The Inn at six o'clock. We can have dinner afterwards." Dorothy shook her head. The man didn't give up.

"Quentin, as soon as you get here and get the papers out and ready, I will allow my new lawyer to go through them and then I will sign if he finds them acceptable." There was a pause as Quentin reviewed his options.

"All right, that will be fine, Dorothy. Until I see you tomorrow, then." His voice was silky smooth as he hung up the phone.

Dorothy almost threw the phone through the window as she let out a frustrated yell. Temperance and Tiffany came running in through the office door.

"What is it? What's happened?" Temperance demanded as Maria made her appearance with the cast iron frying pan in her raised hand ready for battle. The scene was so ridiculous, it made Dorothy smile. She began to laugh as she stood up from the desk.

"You should see yourselves standing there. It's hilarious." Dorothy couldn't contain her laughter. Maybe it was her nerves, but she began to laugh so hard her stomach started to hurt. The laughter seemed contagious as all four ladies realized it had been a funny scene.

Maria waved away the laughter as she lowered the frying pan and returned to the kitchen. Tiffany accompanied her and Temperance went to Dorothy and gave her a light hearted hug.

"It's good to see you laugh again, my dear. I was worried the family business was getting to be too much for you. And after only a week. You are not eating, I can hear you pacing in your bedroom at night, and your temper has been quite evident of late."

"I'm sorry, Mother. I just have a few things on my mind and it has been getting a little hard to concentrate on the family business. But I think the deal I proposed to Quentin Tallas and approved by the family last night is really going to be a good thing. Despite his lack of human emotion, I believe the hotels we sold to him is a good deal. We could no longer keep them maintained, and he has a good reputation where hotels are concerned." Dorothy explained to her mother.

"Then why are you not eating? Or sleeping?" You can tell your mother, you know." Temperance tried to ease it out of her.

"It's nothing; I will straighten this business matter out and my personal problems should be smoothed out by then as well."

"*Personal?*" Temperance thought to herself. "*I wonder* . . . ." Draping her arm around Dorothy's waist she led her daughter into the kitchen where a spirited coffee break made everyone feel better.

CHAPTER TWENTY-NINE

Matt and Ethan sat across from each other and Matt eyed Ethan with some suspicion. Ethan seemed a little nervous about something. After a little small talk, he cleared his throat and eyed Matt through his mirrored sunglasses.

"So how is Dorothy taking all this in?" Ethan asked.

'*There it is.*' Matt thought to himself. '*He is nervous because he wants to know about Dorothy and he doesn't want me to figure it out.*' Matt leaned back in his chair with a smile on his face.

"I can't talk for Dorothy, she has her own way of handling things." Matt said with a ghost of a twitch in the corner of his mouth.

"You can say that again." Ethan mumbled as he took a sip of his coffee.

"What was that?" Matt cocked his head to one side as if to hear better.

"I said I hope it doesn't rain again." Ethan stated firmly.

"Me too." Matt's amusement was evident as he knew the harder he made it for Ethan to get information from him about Dorothy, the more Ethan was likely to just come right out and state what he wanted.

Ethan paused and took another sip of coffee.

"So how is the family doing with the sale of the hotels?" Ethan tried another tack.

"And how did you know about that?" Matt asked as he leaned forward with interest.

"I have my sources." Ethan answered.

"You better not let Dorothy know about your sources. She's a little on edge right now as it is." Matt said.

"Really? How come?" For a man who was supposed to be the force's best interrogator, Ethan was unable to keep the telling look from his face. Matt laughed outright and couldn't seem to stop. Ethan seemed a little offended by this.

"What are you laughing about?" He demanded.

"Is this 'Ethan Barns, Chief of Police' asking, or 'Ethan Barns, the man' who is falling for my sister asking?" Matt continued to laugh.

"I, I, I, uh," Ethan began to sputter.

"Relax, man, relax." Matt reached over and patted Ethan's shoulder. "I'm just trying to push your buttons." Matt's laughter over Ethan's discomfiture subsided. "Boy, you've been hit hard."

"I have no idea what you are talking about." Ethan's tone became sullen.

"You don't have any idea, do you?" It dawned on Matt just then that Ethan was probably just as confused as Dorothy.

"No, I don't."

"Ethan, I think you should call Dorothy up, ask *her* out for coffee, and ask her these questions yourself. Not as the chief of police, but as Ethan Barns." Matt waited for the idea to sink into Ethan's brain.

"You think she would talk to me?" Ethan queried with a worried look on his face.

"As long as you ask as yourself. Don't put on any airs or revert back to your Chief of Police attitude. She doesn't take shit like that from too many people anymore." Ethan nodded and looked down in misery.

"I guess I will have to do just that." The decision made, Ethan sit straighter in his chair. Matt shook his head again in laughter. *'If these two ever get together, the sparks are really going to fly.'* he said to himself.

CHAPTER THIRTY

Quentin Tallas stared out the window of the Presidential Suite at six o'clock. A call had just come through on the phone that Dorothy Adams and her lawyers were on their way up to the room. Quentin was used to business men in three piece suits, driving BMWs, and hauling around an entourage of accountants, business managers, and lawyers. This one young lady in a small hick town had brokered the best deal he had ever done and he was stumped. Why hadn't he met this young lady before and how was she able to pull the family chestnuts out of the fire as quickly as she did? He hadn't seen it at first, but when his lawyers consulted with him, he was amazed at the logical progression of the deal. His anger at loosing the funds he had invested in the real estate deal with Belknap and Marshall had prompted him to try to hold Dorothy up for more concessions for the employees of the hotels he had just bought. Her stubbornness and lawyers quite impressed Quentin. He made the deal as proposed and began to wonder what kind of a woman Dorothy Adams really was.

A firm knock sounded on the door and Quentin turned to see a beautiful young woman with lose auburn hair down around her shoulders and a hard glint in her eyes walk into the room in front of two silver haired lawyers. Her self confidence in the face of Quentin's knowledge and financial wizardry duly impressed everyone in the room, including Quentin.

"Miss Adams, please, come and sit." Quentin moved forward to shake Dorothy's hand in greeting. "These are my lawyers, and I assume these are your lawyers." Dorothy released his hand as if she had shaken a wet, limp snake.

Everyone sat around a large boardroom table that had been placed in the center of the room for just this occasion. The two Tallas lawyers opened their brief cases and handed copies of the deal to the two lawyers with Dorothy. Dorothy looked up in surprise.

"What, don't I get a copy? I am, after all, the seller." Dorothy inquired as she stared straight at Quentin. Quentin had anticipated Dorothy's request and motioned to one of the lawyers who quickly handed Dorothy a copy with a friendly smile. "Thank you." Dorothy said. The next few minutes were spent in almost total silence while the contracts were being read. Quentin took that time to try and read Dorothy a little better.

From the intelligence reports he had on her, he thought he knew everything about her that he needed to know. Apparently, intelligence reports didn't list everything. They left out the interesting fact that she cared for her employees, and wasn't particularly worried about money. The Adams family had deliberately low balled their asking price for a reason that wasn't readily apparent but Quentin had a suspicion as to why they picked him to buy the family business. It had to do with his dubious business dealings with Jim Marshal and Darien Belknap, two of the most fraudulent people he had ever dealt with.

Quentin had always pushed the edges and skirted the outer edges of business dealings but he had always been ultimately honest. Unorthodox methods and dealings did not mean he was dishonest but he did get more things accomplished than the so called upstanding and straightforward business men in the real estate sector of business. The news was always reporting his nefarious dealings and Quentin remained silent, which had the effect of people always making up their minds about his reputation without even getting to know the real story. Only his lawyers and his employees knew he was a great man to work for. Quentin was still watching Dorothy when she glanced up at him as if she felt his eyes on her.

Quentin boldly smiled and turned to look out the window and Dorothy went back to reading the contract. Quentin watched her reflection in the window and noticed her as a woman at that moment. The gently sculpted chin and jaw line was relaxed. Dorothy's auburn hair that tumbled gently across her shoulders, framed her petite features as effectively as a fine picture frame would a beautiful piece of art. Her dark blue sports jacket, white blouse and blue jeans were all worn with a comfortable nuance that showed itself in her every movement. It showed she was at peace with herself and comfortable in her surroundings. Her beauty did not go unnoticed with Quentin as he struggled to bring himself back to the business at hand.

"Does everything satisfy you?" Quentin inquired as he turned back to the table.

"It does appear to be satisfactory." Dorothy said after inquiring with her lawyers. They nodded and Dorothy picked up the pen on the table to sign.

"Before you sign, may I inquire what you are going to do with that parcel of land that you received in this deal?" Quentin sat directly across from Dorothy as she sat with her pen at the ready.

"You mean, that parcel that Belknap and Marshall conned you into buying with the bogus development permits?" Dorothy inquired.

"You cannot build any commercial properties or houses on that land as it is zoned non commercial. Only the one portion at the far end of the parcel is any good." Quentin was very curious as to why Dorothy had fought to have that land a part of the deal.

"I don't plan on building anything on that land." Dorothy signed the contract with a flourish. "It is going to be developed as a memorial park for Anna Price and her family." Dorothy pushed the contract across the table to Quentin.

"And the parcel at the far end?" He asked again.

"That will be the spot where I build a center for children and teens. I am sure the city council will approve the land for use in this case. Who can resist a memorial park for teens and young adults when this city so badly is in need of a place for the teens to go?" Dorothy's gaze was direct and honest and Quentin nodded his head. He signed the contract and handed it to the lawyers.

"That is a very commendable thing for you to do." Quentin was pleased he had made this deal. The young lady had nerve. "Not many people would do that for a city that turned its back on them so many years ago." Dorothy knew at that moment that Quentin had done his research.

"I would like to donate something towards the development of the park and the center." Quentin said and saw the surprise in Dorothy's deep blue eyes. It flashed quickly but Quentin had seen it.

"I see. And how much would you like to donate." Dorothy said after she cleared her throat.

"I tell you what, you give me an estimate and I will give you 75% of what you need to have it done." Quentin's move had not been a total business move to receive good PR. He did have some concerns for the citizens and his heart wasn't entirely made of stone.

"You will give us 75%?" Dorothy asked in surprise. "Why?" she demanded to know. She didn't want Quentin to blow the entire project up into a big publicity stunt.

"I will give you the funds on the condition that they remain anonymous." He said instead. Dorothy's two lawyers were stunned but Quentin's two lawyers didn't look surprised at all. Dorothy took that to mean that Quentin Tallas wasn't the complete hard-ass he wanted everyone to believe he was.

"That would be acceptable. I will contact you as soon as I have the estimates." Dorothy kept her professionalism intact and shook hands with a very surprising business man.

Dorothy shook hands with the other two lawyers and preceded her own out the door as if she made million dollar deals every day. As soon as they were ushered into the hallway and into the elevator, the three of them let out a collective sigh.

"Wow!" The two lawyers said almost at the same time. "Does he realize how much cash that is going to be and he is just going to give it to us?" Dorothy leaned against the wall of the elevator and pondered it for a moment.

"Yes, I do believe he does. He isn't the terror a lot of people think he is; at least not in this case." The elevator opened and Dorothy stepped into the lobby with a grin on her face. "Donuts anyone?" She called as she headed to the café.

CHAPTER THIRTY-ONE

Dorothy had two donuts to be exact, with a cup of coffee that didn't seem to taste all that well. When she was done at the café she went directly to the bank to check and see if the necessary funds had been transferred into the family account. Her business concluded very successfully, she decided to call Matt and inform him of the successful deal. She used her cell phone as she sat in her car.

"Matt here." He answered.

"Hey Matt, Dorothy here." Dorothy said into the phone.

"Hey, Dot! How did business go today?" He asked with a smile as he finished ringing in a sale with one hand and balanced his phone with the other.

"It was a complete success." Dorothy said and Matt could hear her grin over the phone.

"I guess this means the party is on tonight and the news conference tomorrow?" Matt said. Billy was standing next to him as he helped the next customer in line.

"It's done?" Billy asked excitedly.

"Yes, Billy." Matt laughed. Billy always had enough enthusiasm for anything like a party.

"Woo hoo!" Billy yelled and punched his fist into the air. Dorothy heard him and laughed.

"Tell Billy I expect him to be at the party tonight." Dorothy said into the phone then hung up and started her car. There was so much to do and so little time to do it. She drove a couple of blocks over and went into the flower shop that was locally owned by a lovely couple and bought two dozen red stemmed roses.

Dorothy entered the front door of the Manor with the roses in her arms and went straight to the library where her mother was comfortably seated in front of the fireplace. A fire had been laid for later but remained unlit as the warm late summer sun still provided plenty of light and warmth. Temperance looked up from her book and her jaw dropped in surprise.

Dorothy went straight to her mother and gently placed the roses into her arms.

"These are for you, Mother." She said.

"My gosh, Dorothy, whatever did I do to deserve this?" Temperance observed the beautiful flowers in awe.

"For understanding why it was important for us to finish with the family business and move on to our own business; and for supporting me in everything I do." Dorothy sat beside her mother. Temperance's hand reached out to touch the jawline of Dorothy's face and her eyes shone with love.

"It's done?" She asked.

"Yes, mother. Now let's go put those in water and get ready for the party." Dorothy helped her mother up and they went into the kitchen where Maria oohed and awed over the roses.

"Now we party?" Maria asked with a smile.

"Now we party!" Dorothy exclaimed.

"Good! I will get the menu started." Maria turned to her stove.

"No, Maria. You don't have to cook for this one." Dorothy put her hand on Maria's as she reached for the frying pan. "You get to party too."

"Why, don't you like my cooking?" Maria felt like she had been insulted.

"I do love your cooking, but as part of our family, you deserve to join the party, this time. You don't have to cook for it." Dorothy sat the frying pan back down on the stove. "I am having it catered. It won't be as good as yours, but at least you will be able to join the party." Maria smiled and released the frying pan.

"Okay. I will go and get cleaned up." The excitement caught in Maria's chest as she looked around and smoothed her apron. "No cooking for me tonight!" She cried as she took off her favorite apron and went out the back door to go home and clean up.

Dorothy and Temperance looked at each other. Temperance set the roses on the middle of the table in the kitchen with a smile.

"These are for the family and the family only." Temperance said. "Now, let's go and get ready."

The guests started to arrive around seven in the evening. The caterers had already set up in the kitchen and were driving Maria stark raving mad at how they treated her kitchen. At one point, Dorothy had to hide the frying pan and ban Maria from the kitchen altogether. Tiffany had done a fabulous job of cleaning the past few days and everything seemed to shine with a light the house had not seen in a very long while. There was an excitement and happiness in the air that was catching. It increased ever so slightly when Billy arrived to sweep Tiffany up in his arms and swing her around with laughter.

Guests were milling everywhere and the Mayor arrived with his wife. He had a slightly confused and harassed look on his face but he seemed affable enough. Rumor had it someone had punched his ticket in council chambers for being such a jerk and it had taken some of the wind out of his sails. Of course, when he walked in sporting a huge shiner in his left eye, Dorothy had to try very hard not to laugh.

The doorbell rang again almost as soon as the door closed and Matt answered it this time. In through the door walked Ethan Barns, dressed in jeans, t-shirt and sports jacket, complete with cowboy boots and his big buckle. This time a breath caught in Dorothy's throat as she gazed at him from where she stood. Matt greeted Ethan and motioned for him to come in when Ethan looked up and his gaze locked with Dorothy's. Both of them froze for a moment and Matt looked around to see what had caught Ethan's attention.

"Now if that isn't a Kodak moment or what." Matt slapped Ethan on the shoulder and broke the spell. "When are you going to ask her for a date?" Matt cajoled Ethan with a little good natured ribbing on his part.

"Huh?" Ethan started. "Oh, ah, do you really think she would go out with me?" Matt looked at Ethan and laughed.

"I saw the way she just looked at you. I would bet she would be very mad at you if you didn't ask her out." Matt's words instilled some confidence in Ethan as he slowly made his way over to where Dorothy stood talking to one of the city councilors on the developing committee.

"Hello, Miss Adams, how are you this evening?" Ethan tried to be professional and not show his nervousness at that moment. It didn't work. The city councilor nodded at Dorothy with a smile and moved on to where Temperance stood.

"Hello, Ethan. I thought we were on a first name basis." Ethan was encouraged at that and smiled back at Dorothy. Dorothy's tummy clenched and she felt like curling her toes again.

"Can you do me a favor?" Dorothy asked as she led Ethan over to the window seat where the two of them could talk.

"Sure." Ethan said as he sat down beside her. "What can I do for you?" His stomach was beginning to clench as well and a funny feeling in his chest was making itself known.

"Do you get stomach cramps, toe cramps, dizziness, and breathlessness when I walk into the room?" Dorothy's directness startled Ethan. But he liked it.

"Yes I do." He admitted with a smile. "As a matter of fact, I was going to ask you the same thing."

"You were?" Dorothy's smile teased as she laughed. Ethan nodded.

"I guess this means you are going to ask me out, right?" Dorothy surprised Ethan yet again with the direct question. *'This could be a very interesting party.'* He thought to himself.

The music was light and happy and as the sun went down on the Manor, people who were at the party couldn't remember when there had been a better time.

Ethan had found out from Matt and various other family members what the deal was that Dorothy had brokered between Quentin Tallas and the Adams family. And while it hadn't been made official, Ethan knew it was a big coup and put a big feather in Dorothy's cap. The teen center and memorial park would go a long way towards soothing the hurts that had happened because of one unchangeable moment in the town's history. Looking across the room he saw Dorothy talking to the Price family and how they reacted to the news with pride and warmth for the decision. Dorothy could have made things worse but she chose to heal the hurts of a community and choosing to help. Even the actions of a large real estate developer like Quentin Tallas had surprised everyone. Though the city developers didn't know about the anonymous donation, Ethan did and he knew the business deal would be good for the city as well.

People had begun to straggle towards the door and the caterers began to pack up their things when a scream came from the kitchen. Everyone paused for an instant and looked towards the kitchen door. In that instant of immobility, the door opened and Darien Belknap entered the room with his arm around Temperance Adams' throat and a gun held to her temple. Everyone gave a gasp as they were caught flat-footed at the turn of events. The entire room froze.

Temperance's hands clutched at Darien's arm as she struggled to breathe and loosen the grip on her windpipe. Darien's disheveled appearance gave him a wide eyed desperation as he glared around the room.

"Nobody move!" He screamed. Dorothy started to move forward as did Matt and Ethan. Ethan even reached for his gun in his shoulder holster.

"Not gonna happen, cop!" Darien yelled. "Everyone but you get down on the floor. Now!" The fear on Temperance's face tortured Dorothy as she did what she and everyone else was told to do. "Now, Barns, slowly reach into your holster and remove the gun by two fingers. Go slow. I will fire." Belknap threatened. Ethan had no choice and he moved to do as instructed. Belknap's gaze swept the room as he watched for movement from the other hostages. There were only family members and the odd caterer left. Billy began to fidget on the floor.

"You! Billy. Don't move." He screamed.

"Okay, okay!" Billy complied. Belknap moved himself and Temperance forward a foot as Ethan slowly placed his gun on the floor and stepped back.

"Get over there, away from the gun." Belknap motioned with his own for Ethan to move away so he could scoop up the gun.

"You'll never get away with this, Belknap." Ethan's voice was stern and cold. "If you hurt anyone, I swear, I will kill you."

"Shut up!" Came the high pitched scream. Looking at Dorothy he screamed at her. "Where's the money?"

From her spot on the floor, Dorothy tired to answer. "What money?" Her voice was muffled.

"The money you got from Tallas today for the sale of your family's holdings. I want it. You owe it to me and I want it now!" He screamed at her.

"Darien, the money is in the bank." Dorothy answered carefully.

"I want it! Go get it now." In Darien's deranged mind, he didn't realize the futility of demanding the money from the cash transfer. "Get me the check!"

"Dorothy can't get . . ." Temperance tried to answer but Belknap cut her off with a twist of his arm. "You shut up, lady. Your family has done enough damage to this city. I don't need your uppity attitude. I just need your money!" He screamed into her ear. No one heard or saw the stealthy approach of a quiet figure from behind Belknap coming from the direction of the kitchen.

"Darien, the money wasn't in the form of a check. It was a money transfer. It will take time, but I can get it. Please! Don't hurt my mother." Dorothy called out from the floor. Ethan caught his breath in surprise as the shadow moved directly behind Belknap.

"I don't care how long it takes to get it!" Spittle came from Belknap's mouth as he worked himself into lather. "Go get it now!" Darien pointed his gun at Dorothy and in that moment, the shadow behind Belknap brought the frying pan down on the back of Darien's head. Temperance screamed, Belknap collapsed, and Maria looked down at the inert form of Darien Belknap with contempt.

"You filthy pig!" Maria spit at him and raised the frying pan again as if to strike a second time. Ethan reached her in time to take the frying pan away and handcuff Darien as Matt, Dorothy, and the rest of the family came to Temperance's aid.

"I told him I would teach him a lesson that day in the supermarket!" Maria yelled.

Billy took Maria to the side as Tiffany ran to get a glass of water and a cold cloth. Ethan called for backup and an ambulance as Temperance was lowered onto the couch in front of the fireplace.

"Oh Mother. Are you okay?" Matt asked. Everyone had gathered around with concern as they saw the bruises on Temperance's throat. Tiffany came back with the water and the cloth so they sat Temperance up to drink the water. The cold cloth was settled on her throat to help with the pain.

"I will be fine. I'm just a little bit shook up." Temperance looked up as Belknap was carted away by two deputies to be put in the wagon. Looking around, she saw Maria's concerned face along with the others.

"Oh, Maria! You could have been hurt badly." Temperance had to whisper. "Why did you do it?"

"You are my family. You would have done it for me." Maria answered matter-of-factly. "But I think I am going to need a new frying pan." There was a soft swell of laughter at Maria's answer and the ambulance pulled up. Temperance was taken to the hospital and Matt and Brent went with her. Ethan stayed to make out the report and take statements. It was several hours before the task was completed.

Ethan saw Dorothy sitting at the desk in the office with her head in her hands and quietly entered the room, clearing his throat so Dorothy would know he was there.

"Quite a busy day for you." Ethan said. Dorothy's face was drawn and colorless as she nodded.

"Yes it was. But at least it will be over soon." Dorothy agreed. "Tell me, did you find out where Belknap had been hiding?"

Ethan nodded and consulted his notes. For the next few minutes Ethan explained how Belknap had been staying at the local Provincial Park with Jim Marshall in a camper they had borrowed from the family compound. An argument ensued between the two of them when Belknap found out about the sale of the company business through a business contact. He wanted to take the money and run and Jim Marshall wanted to wait until the search for them was called off before they made their move. Belknap won the argument by strangling Jim the same way he had strangled Anna Price. Then he had driven into the city and waited for his chance to make his move.

Dorothy shook her head and began to cry. The emotional turmoil and terror of the past few hours had lowered Dorothy's strength of will. Ethan moved forward and gently took her into his arms.

"Dorothy, sweetheart, it's all over now. Hush." Ethan tried to soothe her tears.

"I'll cry if I want to cry!" She mumbled into his shoulder. Ethan chuckled to himself as he held her tighter. It was going to be an exciting life with someone like Dorothy by his side, but then, he wouldn't have it any other way.

Edwards Brothers Malloy
Oxnard, CA USA
July 1, 2014